First published in Great Britain in 2008 by Comma Press
www.commapress.co.uk

First published in Berlin as *Lange Tage* by S. Fischer Verlag, 2003.

A CIP catalogue record of this book is available from the British Library.

ISBN   1905583028
ISBN-13   978 1905583027

With the support of the Culture Programme (2007-2013) of the European Union.

This project has been funded with support from the European Commission.
This publication reflects the views only of the author, and the Commission
cannot be held responsible for any use which may be made of the information
contained therein.

The publisher gratefully acknowledges assistance from the Arts Council England
North West.

Set in Bembo 11/13 by David Eckersall
Printed and bound in England by SRP Ltd, Exeter

LONG DAYS

by
Maike Wetzel

Translated from the German by
Lyn Marven

Contents

Witnesses

Recently something funny happened. There was no summer, no autumn either. It turned straight into winter. No sooner had the trees blossomed than they dropped their leaves, and in the shops the only vegetables were imported. People did claim that there had been a summer, but I hadn't noticed it. It must have been some kind of mass hypnosis. I was the only one who was not affected. But I didn't feel at all relieved. I wandered around waving my arms, pointing at the bare branches. No-one took any notice. Yards ahead of me people drew aside like supermarket doors. I didn't make any attempt to speak to anyone. I kept thinking about the corpse.

In the darkness of the wood I nearly stumbled over the body lying in the leaves. The soles of my shoes trod on something soft. The flame from Marcel's lighter cast some light on the ground. A boy was lying in the leaves in front of us. His face was ashen and distorted. His eyes were wide open and stared unseeing, the brown iris swimming in milky white. Although he was lying flat on the ground his dark hair seemed to be standing on end in shock. I didn't dare touch the boy, or attempt first aid. Marcel didn't touch him either. He said he must be dead. It was impossible to imagine that this body had been alive just a minute ago. But that's how it had been. A minute ago he had been sitting at the wheel of a black Corsa and had been roaring along a country road. The car was now a crumpled heap of tin. It had concertina folds. All the windows were shattered. From the passenger seat came groaning. A girl with dyed-red hair was hanging doubled-over in her seatbelt. We couldn't help her, the car was too mangled. The door was stuck. On the back seat were a couple, a boy and a girl. They leant against each other. Their faces were peaceful, pale and young. They looked like they were sleeping. Later I heard that they had died on impact.

Marcel called the police. There was a phone box in the next village. We had only heard the accident. Marcel's car was parked on a track in the wood. We were standing by a tree, a bit away from the road, when the Corsa with the four young people hit the beech tree behind us. It spun around once and came to a halt with the bonnet facing forward at a right angle to the road. The driver was thrown out. He was nineteen years old. I read that in the newspaper. The police were looking for possible witnesses and suspected that there had been another car going the other way. We had fled the scene. Marcel had given the emergency services a false name. No-one would ever connect us to the black Corsa.

Even later on we never went to the police to give statements. Although we knew that we weren't guilty. We hadn't been on the road. No-one had been going the other way. There hadn't been a second car. No-one had the youths on their conscience. It was illogical that we had fled. Marcel said he hadn't thought when the woman on the other end of the emergency line had asked for his name. 'Jens Vierwald' was my nickname for him. It had come out quite naturally. After fleeing we were doubly suspicious. A retrospective statement would have been unpleasant. We didn't want to reveal anything anyway, not our names, our families, our friends. No-one knew we were seeing each other. That's how it should stay. Many years later I told Laurenz about it. He asked if I loved him, that boy, Marcel, that I was with then. I said no. It wasn't true, but I couldn't say I didn't know what the feeling was between

2

Marcel and me. It was often flat and wrong, but it was there. Laurenz wouldn't have understood that that was a good thing. So I said I had loved him at first, a bit. By the time we saw the accident I didn't any more. Laurenz's face suggested that was a crime. I said it was all quite harmless.

We were leaning against a tree. Marcel had chased me there; we often played tag. I could feel the bark against my shoulder blades. Our faces were close but weren't touching yet. I pulled up his T-shirt and discovered scratches on his chest. They weren't from my nails. I could picture who he had spent last night with. He had been at his girlfriend's. Playfully I threatened to beat him if he came like that again, flayed by someone else. He grinned and asked if I would keep my promise. He made it sound like he wanted to be beaten. He lunged at me, but I got out the way and called him a cheat, teasingly. He caught my wrist and pressed it against the tree with his right hand. I stopped making his life so difficult. As he bent over my stomach I saw the lights of the car approaching. They were still far away. But over the dark plain I could clearly make them out. I saw the headlights through the trees. I wasn't paying attention to them. Just a car. Marcel's hands fumbled at my belt, I closed my eyes. The collision of the car made a thud. Not loud at all, more dull than a bang. It immediately went silent again. The headlights had disappeared.

We had no idea what had happened, I said. Laurenz said nothing. But you're lying, he stated finally. He didn't seem to be particularly surprised by my dishonesty. He opened the fridge and the light from the bulb in the freezer compartment lit him from below. His gaze travelled along the shelves. He knew exactly what was there. Ham, tomato puree, leeks. He didn't need to open the fridge. He just didn't want to look at me. I said, fine, I'll tell you the whole story.

The boy with the black Corsa was called Arslan. He lived in the next village. I used to watch him from afar at events in the sports hall. I only saw him up close at a party in the bridgehead on the Rhine. Arslan was broad, but solid like a wrestler. I noticed when I bumped into him in the crush. He was wearing a red T-shirt with a James Bond print. Back hair peeked out of the collar at the back of his neck. His eyes were round and dark, I didn't see any white. They observed curiously, surprised. His nose was a short straight block, with no tapering. His face looked open, curious in conjunction with his bear's body. When I bumped against him I could feel he had been sweating, probably for hours. He smelled sour. I had jostled against him while dancing. That happened all the time here – the space in the bridgehead wasn't big enough. I wanted to carry on dancing, but Arslan took me by the elbow and apologised for my jostling. We both knew it was my fault, but he played the contrite party. He bought me a daiquiri. I smiled at him, then turned my back on him. He stood right behind me. With pursed lips I sucked the red strawberry slush through the straw. As I did so my bottom brushed against the zip on Arslan's trousers, as if by accident. Nodding my head I watched the people dancing in front of me, like I had forgotten Arslan was there. I smiled. I was enjoying the evening. Arslan ran his forefinger across my naked shoulder. I ignored that, too, swayed to the music and soon danced away from him. The party finished at six in the morning. The organisers packed away the floodlights. Katja knew the DJ and we all went together to a bungalow in the suburbs. Arslan just came along. He had bought all the roses the Bangladeshi rose-seller had left over for a ludicrous price and had given them to me and Katja. Mine lay on the back shelf. I drove. In the rear-view mirror I could see Katja carefully feeling the thorns on a rose. Arslan was sitting in the passenger seat. We had the radio on. The DJ and Katja couldn't hear us. Arslan said, you're beautiful, you look a million dollars. I asked why dollars? I didn't take him seriously. Arslan said because

4

deutschmarks sounds stupid. I nodded. Arslan admitted that he hadn't invented the phrase. He had read it somewhere. I said I had heard better. He opened his mouth to speak and then shut it again. The road came to a fork. The DJ shouted to me to take the road on the right. He had his hand on Katja's thigh.

The garden of the bungalow was piled up with dirty red wine glasses and cigarette butts. In the evergreen leaves of a holly-bush hung a woollen sock. I couldn't see anyone that it might belong to. The front door was open. The bungalow seemed to consist of one huge living room. You could see that it had been knocked through and that there had previously been several rooms. On the parts of the wall that protruded the brickwork was exposed, the walls next to them were carefully covered with woodchip wallpaper. A lad wearing headphones stood in front of three turntables, which were all going round. He was mixing the music that resounded in the empty living room. It was banging club music, ear-splittingly loud. Framed posters of Chagall paintings hung on the walls. The lad wasn't paying any attention to us. Katja, the DJ and I sat down on the sofa in front of him. The music hurt my ears, the air stank sourly of alcohol and old smoke. Katja's DJ strained to follow the beats. He ground his back teeth. I could see his cheeks moving. The lad wearing headphones was sixteen years old at most. He was lost in his records. Arslan had been silent since the conversation in the car. He had sat down on a leather cube and was making notes. It looked over-eager, put on for effect. I briefly had the feeling that he was the researcher and we were the animals. I grinned to myself. At some point he stood up and went onto the patio. We could see him through the panoramic window. He was just standing there, staring into the Rhine valley. It was a misty morning. We seemed to be cut off from the world. You couldn't make out the river. As always we were waiting for something to happen. We had been the last in the bridgehead, we were the last ones here. Something had to transpire.

Katja reckoned I should go out and join Arslan. The DJ stroked her legs in their shiny golden leggings, lost in thought. I shook my head. I said, What would I do out there? I didn't fancy standing next to a know-it-all wrestler and staring into the mist. I was pretty sure that Arslan would come in. I sank back into the cream-coloured sofa and watched the lad on the turntables doing his stuff. The DJ said that the lad had already produced six albums which were even selling in England. To me the records sounded like a car mechanic's, hammering and knocking, hardly any harmonies. I said nothing and nodded appreciatively. At some point the police came and we left. The neighbours had complained about the music. Arslan hadn't said a word. He had stood on the patio by himself the whole time. His face was damp from the mist.

I took the way home via the villages. The landscape disappeared into grey a hundred yards all around us. The DJ and Katja got out first. The DJ shared a post-war house next to the plexiglass factory with four other blokes. Katja had known him for a while, but she had never stayed the night with him. She winked at me as she got out. Arslan lived with his family in a three-storey block in the new houses. He said goodbye by kicking me in the rear wing. I had just turned the ignition when I saw him kick the car. I put it in reverse and started back in his direction. Arslan swore and jumped out the way. I looked in the rear-view mirror once more and drove off.

That night I had a dream. I won a competition I hadn't even entered. The prize was a ride on an elephant. The elephant had bad breath and Arslan's eyes. I didn't want to get on its back. But I ended up on the straw mat which functioned as a saddle all the same. It was exactly the same mat that I usually took to the swimming pool. It had no grip and slipped around on the elephant's back. I knew that I would fall off at any moment. I was afraid of hitting the ground. The elephant stomped on and I tried to squeeze my thighs tight. It didn't occur to me to hold on.

Did you recognise Arslan, Laurenz asked. No, he wasn't recognisable any more after he'd flown through the Corsa's windscreen, I replied. There was very little light, he looked completely different, I didn't know that death changes people so much. Laurenz wrinkled his nose to hoist up his glasses which had slipped down. There's a lot you don't know, he said. What about the other bloke, the one who was with you? Marcel, I said. He was called Marcel. Laurenz didn't believe that either. He hadn't heard me say the name before. He said, you can call him what you like, so long as you tell the truth about everything else. I countered that I could only tell him what I thought I heard. He said, I don't want philosophising. I just want to know what happened. He stuck his chin out and I knew he wanted an answer. But not to the question he had asked.

After the evening in the bridgehead I spent three months in America. The school exchange had been planned for a long time. I was far away from the Rhine, from the smoky bungalows and the country roads. Arslan wasn't part of the German school group in the United States. When I came home at Easter I read his name in connection with athletics tournaments. He had won the hurdles. I thought about him kicking my rear wing and told my friends sitting at a café table that the hurdler with the medal round his neck, the one in the photo, had once smashed my indicator light, I didn't know why either. Just like that, when I'd dropped him off at home just to be friendly. Nazi pig, he'd called me. They all shook their heads, said 'typical', and in time I believed the story myself.

I told it to Marcel and his girlfriend too. I had known the two of them for a long time by then. Marcel's girlfriend

7

was pretty, colourful, clever. She spoke with a light, soft voice. It sounded falsely obliging. Falsely because she wasn't. She was hard on herself. I felt sorry for her. I knew she would have hated me for my pity and because of our cheating. If you carry on wearing such low-cut tops I won't be able to control myself much longer, Marcel said to me behind her back. We had been sleeping together for a year. Before that we had only managed to touch each other surreptitiously. Sometimes we went to the cinema, the three of us. Marcel sat in the middle.

Arslan had a girfriend too by the time I came back from America, Miriam. They met just two weeks after I dropped him off at his house in the early hours and he had kicked my wing. Miriam went to the same school as me. After my US -trip I often saw her and Arslan together in the schoolyard. Miriam had a ruffled pageboy cut, blow-dried upside down every morning. She wasn't tall, she came up to Arslan's chin. Her torso was thin, she had hardly any bust, but her hips stuck out. In a strange way this disproportion looked good, obscene. My girl friends and I stared at Arslan and Miriam when they wandered off away from everyone else at break. They were more determined than the rest, walking hand in hand, suggesting eternal happiness, along the edge of the school grounds. People talked about them a lot. Arslan had been driving Miriam to orchestra practice for five months, Miriam hadn't looked at another boy for five months. One time I was standing smoking by a bush that the pair suddenly stopped behind. Through the branches I could make out occasional movements. I heard everything. They whispered incoherent sweet nothings to each other. He cried out quietly when she touched him under his clothes. Her hands were too cold for him. He rubbed her fingers warm between his own. After that I only heard the rustling of clothing, sighs and slurps. I crept away. Miriam wasn't at Arslan's funeral. She was in hospital. She was the only one who survived the accident. It was her dyed-red hair that Marcel and I had seen in the passenger seat. It was an artificial dark red. The tint was called Aubergine.

It was true that I hadn't recognised Arslan after he had flown through the windscreen. But I recognised his car. He had bought it off my sister's boyfriend. The fake zebra fur seat covers were home-made, and there was a Greenpeace sticker on the rear window. I knew who the driver was. I stared at Arslan, his ashen, distorted face. I tried to understand what had happened. This moment seemed to be real, the darkness, the wood, the leaves, Arslan's twisted body lying on top. My stomach went into spasms. Marcel dragged me away. I struggled free from him, then I threw up. In the sick I could see tiny bits of lime from my caipirinha. We got into Marcel's car and drove away with the windows wound down. Stomach acid burned in my throat. Outside the black and white edges of the road and the cats' eyes hissed past. Marcel looked straight ahead, he drove as if he was in a trance. It was a clear night.

I thought about the morning mist, that time when Arslan had been sitting next to me in the car. I hadn't told either Marcel or my friends in the café that I hadn't driven straight to Arslan's house after Katja and the DJ had got out of my Kadett. Katja's mother had thought her daughter was sleeping at mine. But she found out the truth by the following Monday. Our mothers went to the same exercise class. Katja got into trouble. But that was later.

Arslan was sitting next to me in the passenger seat, his feet up on the dashboard; he was quiet. The minute Katja and the DJ were gone I turned to him and said in a sweet voice, it's too late to sleep. For a moment he seemed surprised, then annoyed, finally he grumbled in agreement. We drove to a diner on Bundesstraße. The silver table top separated us and I had no idea when I would ever come down. I talked without stopping. I told Arslan whatever came into my head. About my aunt who had been an alcoholic, her disabled son, which everyone thought was her fault, though no one knew any more if she had been drinking back then. My cousin was thirty-five now. He couldn't speak and only showed interest in eating and his cassette recorder in turn. I told Arslan that I was in love with a bloke who didn't know what to do about it, and how much that hurt. I wasn't sure who I meant. Marcel or someone else that I had just met recently. I liked Arslan's sympathetic face. When I came back from the toilet I squeezed in next to him on the red vinyl bench. I rested my head on his shoulder and at some point the waiter asked us to leave. I had already seen half of Arslan's tattoos, his T-shirt rode up over his navel, my skirt was twisted.

In the car, driving, we carried on fumbling, until we were in front of Arslan's house. I pulled up and he said, come with me. I played hard to get. Nah, rather not. Arslan insisted, his room was right next to the front door, no one would see anything. I said, will you promise me something? He said yes, and I asked him not to hurt me. I said that I'd had my heart broken so many times before, the next time would be the end. He looked at me and said, what do you mean by that? I replied meaningfully, just like that. Over. Out. End of. Every farewell took a little part of me. I couldn't bear it to happen again, I'd fall apart. The next time. Arslan pursed his mouth. For a moment I was afraid he would tell me not to talk such rubbish. But he took me in his arms, my head was on his chest, he stroked my back and that's when it started. I shook and gasped and couldn't stop. After a while Arslan finally noticed that I wasn't crying. He pushed me away and I wiped the tears of laughter from my face. The next moment he stormed out of the car. I turned the engine on, and he kicked the wing. I started back, he sprang to one side, swearing. I grinned and drove off. After 20 yards I stopped and chucked his wallet out of the car window. The coins rolled into the gutter. I waved to him in the rear mirror.

After that I only watched Arslan from afar, I always saw him together with Miriam. He looked right through me. I never said hello to him. It didn't seem real that we'd kissed. I couldn't believe it myself any more. Until the moment in the wood, when he was lying at my feet, dead. I had nearly stepped on him in the dark. At that moment I was scared, although nothing was threatening me. My stomach went into spasms.

I rubbed my temples as I told Laurenz about it. I knew exactly why I hadn't gone into the house with Arslan, why I hadn't wanted to walk with him across the schoolyard like Miriam, why I had laughed just when it was getting serious. I had done it because I could, because he let me. But in the face of the smoking wreck and the corpse on the ground I had pangs of conscience. Laurenz said, you had nothing to do with Arslan's death. It was a slippery road, drunkenness, fooling around or just bad luck. No, I said. It wasn't any of those. His voice sounded irritated. What was it then? Oil? Animals? Brake failure? Sudden loss of consciousness? I tried to remember what Arslan's friends had told me. I hadn't asked too many questions, that would have looked suspicious.

They had been to a club. Arslan, Miriam and the couple on the back seat. Arslan watched Miriam dancing, probably just like he had watched me in the bridgehead, the year before. The smoke from the machine burned his eyes. Arslan drank one beer after another. By the end he was drinking other people's pints. He just didn't get drunk. A week beforehand Miriam had finished with him. It was the first time they had seen each other since, Arslan and her. The previous week Arslan had eaten nothing but crispbread and chocolate, and drunk tap-water. He had cried, insensible, for hours. He'd thought about calling Miriam a dozen times before he actually did it. They arranged to go dancing. Arslan acted indifferent the whole evening. She avoided meeting his gaze.

I don't know exactly what happened in the car. Some people think Miriam said something, Arslan got angry, he let go of the steering wheel, either to show off or out of anger, they tussled. I don't believe it. The Corsa was heading straight for the beech tree. I saw the headlights over Marcel's back. There weren't any skidmarks. I think the idea came to Arslan quite suddenly. He wanted to stop Miriam getting out. He wanted the pain to stop. Maybe the idea was only strong enough for one moment. The moment when he gripped the steering wheel more firmly and hit the accelerator. The one person who was supposed to die with him survived. Miriam was badly injured. Arslan died, as did the two on the back seat, Felix and Illeana. It was sheer chance that they were sitting there. They had only wanted a lift. In that moment Arslan had probably forgotten they were even in the car.

I lost a whole summer, and autumn too, because of the image of the young people in the accident. That's how long I couldn't think of anything else and I didn't even notice. The sunflowers bloomed, the ferris wheel was put up in the town for the harvest festival, my father broke his arm. Even as these things were happening they already seemed like memories to me. I tumbled through clouds of midges, mountains of leaves, but I didn't see anything. Marcel had disappeared too. It was a strange, airless time. I'm happy that it passed. I finally managed to drive the dead out of my mind the following winter. Many years later I told Laurenz this story.

I reached for his hand and forced him to look at me. I said, you're the first person I've told this to, no one else knows about it. Actually I had already whispered the story once before. Miriam was being kept in an artificially-induced coma when I visited her. She couldn't have heard me speaking quietly. The machines in the intensive care unit had drowned me out. I didn't tell Laurenz about it. He closed his eyes and breathed deeply.

Shadows

We are eating at the round table. The lamp hangs down low. Around us are black windows. It's dark outside. The neighbours can see us, we can't see the neighbours. I switch the television off. It's at the other end of the room. A click, a flash, the picture collapses.

It is quiet. The basketwork on the chair creaks when I sit down. The silver platter is covered with cold meats, the sausage has bits in. I reach for the bottle of water. My father passes it to me. I pour myself a glass, little bubbles rise in the water. The plastic bottle pops back into shape. I jump. The napkins are dirty from yesterday. There is caraway bread, salami, radishes. Our evening meal. My father places a piece of holey Edam on a slice of bread. He leans over the plate, takes a bite, bites again and swallows the food down. My mother spreads margarine on her bread. She picks up the sausage with her fork. She pulls off the yellow skin, cuts the sausage to fit, places it on the bread, with chives on top. She takes a bite, chews and swallows. Soon she'll burp. Heart burn. I fish for gherkins with my fork. They are swimming among the mustard seeds and fronds of dill, like pond water in a glass, gherkin frogs. I bite a gherkin, suck. My father looks up. I bite the gherkin into pieces using my back teeth. My mouth is open a bit as I'm doing it. I make slurping noises. No-one says anything. My sister is staring at the table. She picks up her knife, turns it in her fingers. She has already drunk two glasses of fizzy water. She stands up. My mother asks where

15

she's going. Are you after something? My sister shakes her head. She goes into the kitchen. Her tapered trousers flap around her legs. She is wearing a child's jumper. It's made of acrylic. The material stinks when you sweat. My sister never sweats. I can't see what she's doing in the kitchen. I hear her opening the cupboard and taking something out. The scales rattle as she pours something onto them. The fridge door opens. My sister is probably getting milk. She pours it out. We listen to the sounds. Water flows through the pipes, splashes into the basin. A receptacle is held in the stream, there's probably milk in it. Water to dilute it. My sister comes back, a tray in her hand, a small bowl of muesli on it. She sits down. My parents look at each other; I take more bread. My sister has forgotten her spoon. She says something inaudible. She stands up, disappears into the kitchen. My mother looks decisive, she acts quickly. She cuts a knob of margarine with her knife, she balances the fat on the tip of the knife, but doesn't put it on her plate. She drops it into the muesli. With the knife handle she stirs so that the fat dissolves. My father watches her. My mother can't say anything, my sister will be back any second. My mother folds her napkin. My sister comes to the table. She sits down and pours the red tea into her cup. It's her fourth pot today. She drinks. The bread crumbles in my mouth. My sister doesn't look at us. She stirs the muesli with her spoon. She spots the yellow lump of fat. She stares at it in disbelief. She fishes the margarine out. Her mouth opens, it's starting to form the first letter, then she presses her lips together, the corners of her mouth twitch. She won't cry. She gets up and goes.

My sister won't eat. We don't know why. Her skin lies in folds on her bones. My mother is in despair, my father doesn't let it show.

I go to my room. Out of the window I can see the rented apartment block opposite. Our house is on higher ground, we look onto the roof. One Friday in October, some years ago, my father lifted me over the fence. I played with a girl from the block. Her parents both work on the assembly line in the car factory. I thought that was exciting.

My bed is crumpled. I never make it. What's the point? Toys lie on the mattress. I have sorted them. The toys used to belong to my sister and me, we don't need them any more. Blonde dolls with long legs, angular little figures with no nose, plastic bricks. Barbies, Playmobil, Lego. The usual names from the toy department. For children up to twelve years of age. I am nearly twelve, my sister is fourteen. We don't play with toys any more. I carry the things to the children next door. There you go, we don't have any use for them any more. I don't say: the Playmobile figures have no waist, we're growing up. The children next door grab the play chest, they are pleased. I go home. I look for volume eight of the dictionary. It has disappeared. Advice books are piling up in the living room. My mother reads them like indictments. She wants to cure my sister. We all want it to be over. Shopping seems to be easier than it was before. The options are limited. 'Go ahead' is our main supplier.

Before is a long time ago. I can't remember what it was like any more. Did my sister have friends? Did they dance to old records? Bill Ramsey, the sweetheart from the belly dance troupe. Did they play at brides? With breasts as big as melons? Did the Sultan choose the girl with the biggest ones?

I'm lying on my bed, my toy elephant between my legs. I stare at the ceiling. It's wood panelled. The boards are the colour of honey. Wasps crawl through the knot-holes above me. Every day there are more of them. Today is particularly bad. I'm afraid that they have built a nest. I lie totally still. The wasps fly around my room. One lands right next to me. Its compound eyes are strangely pixellated. New wasps continue to stream out of the black knots above me. I hold my breath. The wasp crawls up the bedcovers towards me. I run for the door, fling it open, yell. My father is in the garden, he comes upstairs. We go back into the room. He closes the door behind him; I stand next to him. We are nearly the same height. The wasps are everywhere. They cover the window, the wall, the bed. There are too many wasps. My father can't do anything about them. Tomorrow a pest controller will get rid of them, the whole colony and their grey honeycombed citadel.

I sleep downstairs, in bed with my mother while my father takes the couch in the living room. My sister doesn't sleep. I hear the floorboards creak above me. She wanders around in her room, moves furniture, reshelves books, orders her records, counts her hairs. They are getting fewer and fewer.

My sister doesn't eat. That's all she does. All day she concentrates on not eating. She says it's like a demon, she can't do anything about it. She summoned it and now she can't get rid of it. She says she wants to eat, but can't. We can't understand, none of us, not even her. In the beginning she was in control, very deliberate, she drew up diet plans, disciplined herself. She did everything possible to shrink. She believed she could turn back whenever she wanted. But now nothing will go down. She is becoming how she feels. My mother is afraid that she will disappear. My father hopes it's just a phase.

My sister tells me fairytales. She likes doing that. She tells me about Beauty and the Beast. Beauty saves the prince, she recognises him under his monstrousness. What would you wish for? I ask. My sister has no idea. She says, something would occur to me, when it came to it. I say maybe she ought to know now. We are lying in bed. I cuddle up to her. She has down on her body, woolly fluff like on premature babies. In the biology book there's an illustration. Babies born too early have fluffy hair on their back, on their shoulders and on their cheeks. It is supposed to keep them warm. The hair is called lanugo. That sounds pretty. My sister makes sure that no one notices the downy hair. She covers up her skin, brushes her hair over her face, to hide the down on her cheeks.

One sunny day I have to take photos of my sister. She calls me into her room, hands me the camera, the little fast one. I say I don't want to. Do it for me, she asks. It's not for a beauty contest. The sound her mouth makes is reminiscent of laughter. She cowers on the carpet, nearly naked, her gaze averted, her knickers hang off her hips. Her shoulder blades are small wings. I press the button.

My mother asks, how was it in school? I slide onto the corner bench next to her. My sister is sitting at the other end of the table. My mother asks us both but she is looking at my sister, who is weighing up the potatoes on her plate with her eyes. Bakes, soups, pudding, my mother hasn't cooked any of those for a long time. There could be all sorts in them, fat, sugar, lard. My sister only eats pudding she has made herself. She takes low-fat milk thinned with water and sweetener and stirs. She refuses dishes that my mother could have hidden fat or sugar in. So my mother cooks everything on view. Everything sits separately on the plate, no sauces. My sister turns the potatoes on her plate over, she pokes in between the beans, every so often she takes a bite. She chews for ever.

Sometimes my mother gets angry, then she bakes. Until the whole house smells of cherry cake, cherry cake with hazelnut sponge. To go with it she makes hot chocolate with cream, proper bitter chocolate, not ready made cocoa powder. I eat and drink everything. I like chocolate most. My sister chucks three sweeteners in her rosehip tea. She sips from the cup and watches us. My mother can't stand it any longer. Her voice becomes hysterical on the phone when she calls my father. He comes home early. She opens the passenger door. My parents drive off to look at castles. They are trying to distract themselves. I sit at home and read.

My sister says something. Her face has disappeared, her mouth has grown too big, with every word her face twists into a grimace. You can't look at it any more. It's indecent. She is ugly. I turn away. She says she was the number one candidate. She had always known that. She has read all the books about starving yourself. They say who is most at risk. Lots of people are. My sister says that all her circumstances pointed towards it. She knows her situation, she knows where all the other cases have led. She gets up at six in the morning, runs around the block, into the wood, to the cemetery. Our grandfather lies there. She always carries ID with her, in case she collapses. But no one can read it in the wood, the paths are empty. On the photo in her child's ID my sister has thick brown plaits. She looks distrusting, squints. Even then she was no beaming cheerleader, her smile is mere politeness. The photo is four years old, today no one would recognise her In it. When she comes back to the house after her run she has a cold shower. Afterwards she is warm for quarter of an hour. It's a mild day today. She doesn't notice. She is freezing, despite the herbal teas from the vacuum flask and three layers of clothes on top of each other. The only clothes hanging in her wardrobe are old, handed down, worn out. New things would be a waste. She wears a jumper from the flea market, one of my father's shirts. My mother insisted she wear the angora underwear. My sister objected to the cost. Her stick-legs disappear in the shaft of her boots, her trousers are wide and padded. She cycles to school. She rubs the skin from her tailbone on the saddle on the incline of the motorway bridge. Every day she finds it harder to climb. But even going downhill she pedals. I take the bus.

The school doctor sends a blue letter to the house. He has weighed my sister, and saw everything. The bruises on her bottom, on her elbows too. Because the bones stick out. She can't sit or lie down. The letter asks whether she is getting treatment, she needs it. The form tutor wants to cure her himself. My sister declines, gratefully. She is on her third therapist already. She wore the first one out straight away. My sister's first therapist wasn't her type. She couldn't stand his ears, his voice, his ideas. It isn't any better with the two new ones. She claims it is, but I don't believe her.

She now has two therapists at the same time. With one of them we all have to go with her to the session. Father, mother, children. The therapist records us. It's always new C60 tapes. He peels the cellophane off, puts the cassette in and then we're off. He speaks. We are supposed to join in. I squint at the recorder's loudspeaker. I don't want to be recorded.

The cassette-therapist wants my sister to leave the second therapist. At some point she does. Although now she doesn't have a therapist to herself any more. Just the cassette-therapist, whom we share, once a month.

We have to tell fairytales for the therapist, everyone tells their favourite. That's our homework. We fight over the books with the Grimms' and Andersen's fairytales. My sister goes to the bookshop and reads Chinese fairytales. She names one that the therapist doesn't know. We are supposed to choose by intuition. I don't know what that means. The therapist isn't pleased with us. Every week when we come into the practice we play musical chairs, we change the order we sit in. The therapist is not to get any hints about our dynamics. The yellow leather sofas squeak under our bums. We can hear it on the cassettes at home. The tapes quickly disappear from the living room, never to be seen again. We don't search for them. The therapist says we should stop thinking about my sister's weight all the time. It's harder to avoid thinking about something than it is to think about something. I have small headphones, round ones. I put them in my ears when it doesn't work, when I'm thinking about my sister again. The woman's voice in the headphones sounds tiny, soft, she's almost whispering, the band sounds like a dance orchestra. At the end of the verse the singer screams, lets rip, gaily. 'Til it's over and then, it's nice and quiet, but soon again, starts another big riot.'

My father loves my mother, my mother loves my father, my parents love us. The therapist says, lovely. He gives us names. I am sunshine. I size the therapist up, look him up and down. He shouldn't think he can suck up to me like that. I look scornfully at his silver glasses, his grey tank top, his worn shoes. His face is expressionless, his voice is calm. My parents want to be punished, if that helps. They would do anything to get my sister to eat. We don't go out any more. Everyone stares. Everyone stares at us. They count our misdeeds on every one of my sister's ribs. We are the Addams Family. Everyone knows what's wrong with us, except us.

At night in bed I run my foot over the knot-holes in the wood panelling. The sloping ceiling above me is full of them. I can't sleep. A floor below me my mother is shouting, I can't hear my father. I know she's shouting, do something, you have to do something. I know he's saying, there's nothing I can do. Putting margarine in muesli doesn't help, if my sister won't eat. My mother is crying. She's afraid that my sister will carry on starving herself. She could destroy everything by starving herself, her body, herself and us as well. My father takes my mother in his arms. He can't comfort her. He is afraid himself. At some point the bedroom door goes and they are quiet. I keep listening. It stays quiet. Something pulls me deep under my sheets. I fall asleep.

My friends don't ask about my sister any more. There's nothing new to say. We read Bravo and phone the sex-problem-helpline. We ask questions which have already been published, the woman at the other end spots it. We hang up, giggling.

Nelly cuts my hair. Afterwards my favourite shirt is itchy. She strokes a powder brush over my eyes, my face, my neck. On the right side my hair stops at chin length, Nelly has left it long on the left. She had a photo from a magazine to copy. She says it's all the rage. I hug her.

For high diving I wear a blue swimsuit and can feel my blond hair glow. The Turkish boys are the prettiest. They have brown eyes. But there are so many of them. They stand on the side of the pool and whistle. A little victory tune. I push away from them and out of the water and quickly check to see whether anything has ridden up. The grass by the open-air pool smells freshly cut.

When I come home it's winter. My sister is baking gingerbread houses. Three of them, one for each of us. Her one from last year is still standing, it has a grey film now. For our houses she makes icing, in every colour. The houses are prettier than our mother's. Her gingerbread comes from a packet. My sister makes her own. She uses three times as much butter as the recipe says. The houses have pointy roofs with hundreds and thousands on top. Hansel and Gretel and the witch come from the supermarket. My sister went to every shop to find the cheapest figures. I want to dig in straight away. My sister says, lick out the bowls. I do it. My sister studies cookbooks and calorie charts. She could become a nutritionist. She doesn't read any other books, apart from books for school. Reading is pointless, it doesn't burn any energy.

I hear my sister behind the wall, lying on the radiator. She bangs against the humidifier. It clanks, I can hear it. I know she's freezing, there on the other end of the central heating pipes. Her blood is slowing, her legs are mottled purple, her hands and feet are dying off.

I have grown again, my sister is shrinking. Sometimes I catch her with a cigarette in her hand. One draw and she nearly falls over, she gets so dizzy. She sucks greedily right into her stomach. She doubles over. Why do you do that? I ask. The dizziness passes, my sister says. I say nothing. My sister doesn't listen to music, she doesn't read, she doesn't watch television, she has no friends.

It is very quiet now in our house, when the neighbour rings it makes us jump. She's bringing rosy-cheek juice. So the child might get better soon. The juice is meant to stimulate the appetite. Because the poor thing isn't hungry. My sister's stomach grumbles. My sister puts the unopened bottle of juice in my room.

My parents and I don't like eating any more, it's no fun. My mother has to cook what my sister wants. My sister says no, please, don't take any notice of me. But what else can we do? My mother hides the scales. My sister agreed, a trial withdrawal. On the third day she cracks up. She isn't even drinking anything out of fear that her stomach might bloat. The scales come back. I press the digital display. The memory shows thirty-one kilos.

At the races we are in the VIP lounge. There is a buffet. My sister sidles up to it. She picks at a plateful. A plateful for her is about as much as I leave on my plate. I take a bit of everything, but leave the meat, it's disgusting. The jockeys hang around the tent with hungry faces. They haven't been yet, they aren't allowed to eat. They have to be light for the horses, I think. They are tiny, wiry lads. One says to me I look like Greta Garbo. I think that's funny, such an old fogey. My father looks over at me suspiciously. He is talking to colleagues. My mother keeps my sister in her sight, she talks to her. The horses thundering by outside don't entertain my mother. The horses have muscles blown up like balloons, big and beautiful. The jockeys become strong when they are on their backs. After the race a waitress goes to the buffet and fills a tray for the riders, they all eat in the stables. All the men in the tent are wearing ties, the women are all wearing stilettos. Their heels bore into the lawn; they lift the turf off the ground. The guests only occasionally look at the screen with the horses' names. The results flicker there, outside people are cheering. My mother is wearing lipstick. She dabs red onto the serviette. She's warm. I don't know why we are here. My sister scratches the insides of her elbows till she bleeds. Her plate is empty. Tomorrow I'll tell everyone that we bet on the wrong horse. It was nice anyway, the weather.

It is spring. The brochures for the sanatorium are lying on the kitchen table, my sister reads them like travel brochures. The sanatorium is expensive and in Austria. The pictures in the brochure are drawings: a white house with cross-bar windows, an entrance with pillars, poplars and a light green lawn, people wander in the garden, sketched pencil schemes. Maybe it doesn't exist. There are no photos in the brochure. My sister dreams of peaceful days in the park. But she doesn't want to allow herself to get a holiday as a reward. She holds out.

In PE we do judo. The boys are gone, in another group, we don't see them. The suits are white, the material is rough and stiff, the sleeves stick out. My jacket has marks on. We learn how to tie the belt. The trainer is not a teacher, he has been hired in. He calls me and demonstrates something. He takes me by the sleeve and the shoulder, like we're dancing, but he grabs hold of the material. He turns with me, pulls me round. I think, this is easy. Then he trips me up, I hit the floor. He says, good, first we will learn how to fall, the way you fall you could break all the bones in your body. I scramble to my feet. The mirrored wall opposite has a dent, I look over at it. My face is distorted and wide like in a soup spoon.

My sister is two years above me, the trainer knows her. He puts her in the judo team. He needs to have people in every weight class, that increases the chances of winning. We go to the county championships, I am just a spectator. Two lads from the team take me in their car. They are twenty already. One of them is the master, the best in the club. He is good-looking. I laugh really loudly; he just keeps on staring ahead.

25

The speedometer nearly hits one hundred and eighty; we are on the motorway. It's hot, the sun glistens on the bonnet. But it isn't the sun which is making us hot. The master has turned the heating up as far as it will go. He is wearing a tracksuit, shiny black and fastened up everywhere, to keep the heat in. He is sweating, so is his friend. He asks, how much further, a hundred kilometres? Will that be enough? The master says sure. If not, we'll just do a few laps in the hall. We'll jog, run to the loo, pee, and back on the scales. If I make my weight I'll eat two sausages, a bar of chocolate and three portions of cereal with full-fat milk. The friend yelps. Please don't talk about eating, it hurts. He is thirsty too, he isn't allowed to drink otherwise it would all have been for nothing. They call it 'making weight'. I put my hands on the seat in front of me and say, you're weird. The lads laugh. The master says thanks. They take it as a compliment.

In the weighing room it's all go. I sit on a wooden bench and watch. Lots of the girls don't make their weight at the first go. It's the same for the boys, but I'm not allowed in their changing room. The trainer comes up to the scales with the little ones. For one six-year-old he grabs her trousers and lifts her slightly. The woman at the scales acts as if she hasn't noticed. The girls over ten strip. They take off their white suit, then their T-shirt, socks, bra, pants, watch, and finally earrings, glasses, hair grips. Yesterday they had a hot bath, drank nettle tea, as a diuretic, then ran to the loo to pass water. Afterwards they didn't drink a thing and hardly ate. If all that didn't help, they will try to jog before the weigh-in. They run round in circles in the hall like prisoners, round the mats which have already been laid out. There is only an hour left before the end of the weigh-in. Some judoka manage a whole kilo in the time. Even after they have lost enough weight by running their thighs won't stop shaking. Later during the fight they are still wobbly on their feet. Their opponent soon grapples them to the ground. The joggers land in a handhold, their opponent's arm goes round their neck and squeezes. They fall down. They don't even manage to give in formally. To do that they would have to slap the palm of their hand on the ground. The umpires are surprised. So many fainting... that's puberty, they say. They are growing too quickly, the body can't keep up.

My sister doesn't have to fight. She stands on the podium alone. No-one is as light as she is. There was only one opponent at her weight, and she had left already after quickly throwing my sister to the ground. My sister chucks the medal down the toilet, I hear it from outside.

After the competition I make fried potatoes. My sister says, Please, let me do it. She shovels butter in, again and again. It takes twice as long for the potatoes to be ready when she does it. They taste greasy. My sister watches while I eat. I lose my appetite. I turn the music up on the radio. My sister pulls a face, the radio is too loud for her. Please, she whispers. Everything is too much for her. The light too bright, the music too loud, there are no people here any more. Our house is dead.

I escape to Paul's. We listen to The Cure, he wears black. We sit in the granny flat in his parents' house, crouching close to each other, till the shadows crawl from the corners. Neither of us puts the light on.

My sister doesn't want to die. She just wants everything to stop, to just go to sleep. If she dies, I'll get her diaries. I'm to burn them, she says. She has got that from Kafka. She doesn't want anyone to find out later how miserable she was. She says there is only rubbish in the books. In her diaries there are also weight tables – the therapist reckoned that would help. The curve slopes downwards, steeply at first, now gram by gram. I peeked secretly. Every day we wait to see if my sister will get up. When she finally appears at breakfast we breathe out again.

The therapist says we should tell our family story. We don't know what that is. My sister explains that he wants to break us. She avoids every question, questions every statement, she sounds tortured, tired. The therapist is like the TV preacher. He talks quietly, knows best. We never meet other people in his practice. We must be the only ones. It's always dark when we arrive.

In the car I put down the armrest between me and my sister. She massages the hunger pressure point on the palm of her hand. She wants to feel hungry again, she says. Her insides have long since stopped complaining. She is beyond hunger. Her hair is like fairy silk, transparent, her skin stretches dully over her bones. Her eyes sink in blueish holes, the edges of her eyelids are red. I ask my sister if she thinks she looks pretty like this. She says no. Do you think you're too fat? I ask. No, not now, not recently. Why do it all then? I don't understand her. Brain-washing, you can't get out of it, my sister says. I ask, what do you want to prove? My sister shakes her head. My mother looks in the rear-view mirror, my father changes into fifth gear.

After every session with the therapist we go for a meal. I find a piece of plastic wrapper in the hollandaise sauce on my asparagus. It's as big as a cigarette packet. I feel disgusted. My sister pokes at her salad. I say there's a wrapper in my food. My mother wants to alert the waiter, my father is against it. My mother calls the waiter over, my father says nothing. We get a chocolate pudding to make up for the plastic wrapper, no one wants it. The pudding stays on the white tablecloth. Little table, spread yourself. The swing doors at the entrance to the kitchen squeak.

My sister can sense starving in other people too. She looks at strangers – boys and girls – and knows. Sometimes she can sense it before it has even broken out; it's like there are underground passages connecting them, or radar. Animals can feel earthquakes coming. My sister feels anorexia. She can read minds, seismographically. She measures the tremors. Generally it's too late by then. In any case, she doesn't do anything to help the others. Sometimes it's adults that my sister points out to me on the street. Some look quite normal.

During break my sister watches a girl from year seven, a bundle of bones with a perm. The history teacher follows her to the toilet. What is he after? My sister avoids all eye contact, she doesn't want to have anything to do with the others. The ambitious girl from the tenth class is also in the club; my sister can't stand her. I find her sad with her red rouged cheeks, Lagerfeld jeans with no bum in them. During the break my sister hugs the radiator. The other pupils are fighting for biscuits from the kiosk. My sister's hands are white as wax, even now in spring.

The girls from my sister's year go to dance class. They have dance partners: tall, blond, brown, suit, jeans, leather jacket, everything. After the dance class disco on Saturday night they make out. The fathers beep impatiently, they are waiting in the car. My sister is never asked. At the leavers' ball she has to dance with a trainee, he gets his ticket paid for. The trainee is huge and fat. She hops in her black tulle dress like a plucked raven to try to keep step with him. The trainee hates her. It's his job to dance with her, but he doesn't like doing it. My sister is tense. The trainee holds his arms away from his body, he keeps his distance from her.

I slurp Coke at my parents' table. A boy asks if I'm dancing. I say no. I can't dance. I tell the next one that my foot is sprained. He asks my parents if he can sit down with us. My mother says please do.

I see the trainee and my sister on the dancefloor; she looks pale, defeated. She isn't looking up. He counts, one, two, three, cha-cha-cha. They fan out like they are supposed to. They hold hands in the middle; their free arms are arched out to the side invitingly. The trainee turns his hips to the side, like a matador making way, my sister's hips are covered in tulle.

I lock the bathroom door behind me. I'm meeting Nelly at three. We want to go swimming; I promised her. The top compartment in the bathroom cabinet belongs to my sister, that's where her tampons and pantyliners are, she has no need for them any more. I take the box of tampons down from the cupboard. I read the instructions then I peel the plastic off and tug once on the light blue string. The tampon sits on my index finger like a thimble made of pressed cotton wool. It's the smallest size, but it still looks big. I can't imagine where it is supposed to go in my body. I know anatomy, but that is just drawings. I take a deep breath and stick my finger with the tampon between my legs. It hurts. I put a leg up on the edge of the toilet. The pain brings tears to my eyes. The tampon won't disappear inside me. I wonder what is wrong, I'm doing everything according to the instructions. My mother wants into the bathroom; she's knocking. The tampon hurts, I chuck it away. I stalk out of the bathroom with my sanitary towel nappy. It bulges at the back and between my legs. The towel is so huge that everyone can see it. The plastic rubs against my skin.

My sister disappears into the bathroom too. She asked my father how the electric razor copes with long hair, where the attachment was, and he told her. Only when she has gone does he realise what she intends to do. He alerts my mother. She knocks on the bathroom door again, she hears the razor buzzing behind the door. My sister doesn't answer. She hasn't locked the door. My mother goes in. My sister is just taking the razor to her head when my mother snatches it away from her. She wanted to shave her head, to stand out, but she didn't manage it. She had been silent in school for three days, hadn't made a sound, not even in class. She wanted someone to notice her, but no one registered her silence, not the teachers, the pupils, her friends from before. Her voice trembles. She says she doesn't have anything to offer, no boy will want a girl who has nothing to offer. Everybody sees her as the ill one, for ever and ever. My mother gets louder. She wants to comfort my sister. I hold my hands over my ears. I can't listen to the shouting.

The gym hall is large and grey, from outside it looks like Noah's Ark. Flagpoles stand in front of the entrance. I don't recognise the flags, none are black red gold, that isn't right. I do trampolining in the gym hall. Finally it's my turn. The other girls stand around the edge of the bed, they rest their arms on top. If I fall, they will catch me. I bounce higher each time. I am so light, my toes are my rocket propulsion, my feathers. In the air I pull my legs in, tuck. I drop down, spring up, pull my legs apart for a straddle, then a turn, and in the next bounce a somersault. The trampoline absorbs me, stretches deep down towards the ground, slings me up in the air. I have to stay in the middle; the edge is dangerous. I'll only be allowed to go there next year. The most important thing in trampolining is to keep tense. I can't let myself go loose. Otherwise I will fly off. People who let themselves go loose break their bones. My trainer, Perry, shattered his foot when he wasn't paying attention. He thought about something else for just one second, maybe he was thinking about his pension, maybe his freshly painted fence, and he stopped tensing, bounced up wrongly, the springs catapulted him from the trampoline. He lay on the floor, his foot twisted, three ligaments were torn, he had a fracture on the ankle bone. He had to be operated on, wasn't allowed to do any sport for six months, wasn't allowed on the trampoline. His leg is thin and white when they take the plaster off. I feel his calf. The leg doesn't look like Perry's, it is thin like a child's. The skin feels raw, hairy. I say, Goodness Perry, how will you bounce with this stick? He says he will bounce on his bum. I smile. He is so old, he can imagine anything. He has done a lot.

Bouncing looks easy; it feels easy. I'm flying. None of the people standing round can hear me groaning because the springs on the trampoline drown it out. From below, bouncing looks effortless, but when I climb down from the trampoline I'm out of breath. My knees give way, the ground seems nearer than usual, my weight is heavy like I'd just fallen down to Earth from the Moon, shocked by gravity. That's how it was after roller-skating too. Rolling over asphalt tickled my feet, recharged them, like a massage. I used to slalom across the street in front of our house. But after roller-skating walking feels like crawling. After trampolining it's the same, but worse.

It's raining on our house; the shutters rattle in the wind that gets in between them. My parents get out the board game. My sister sets out the figures according to colour and size, lines them up in front of her. We throw the dice to see who will go first. We all throw once. But we have forgotten to say whether high or low wins. We start again. My mother says that whoever throws the highest number will start. She throws a five, none of us gets any higher. My sister says well done. Her voice is like her, thin and doleful. She burns into my ear. Before people used to get us mixed up on the telephone, not any more. My sister chirps.

I hear my sister bouncing on the floor above me. She has bought a little trampoline; she is copying me. While she is bouncing she repeats her vocab for French. She looks like a ghost in her white night-shirt. She never changes it, that would be wasteful. My sister moves constantly, she can't stand still, although every step is difficult for her.

It is winter. My sister won't eat. The cassette-therapist said that the shadow would pass after seeing him for three months maximum. That was a whole year ago. My father shakes his head and says that such superstitions don't help, believing in a therapist is wrong. It hasn't gone away. My father tells the therapist that the child can't believe in anything any more, let alone think. His daughter is hazy with starvation, she lives in her own world. Everything revolves around starving herself – we are just shadows to her. He is waiting for her to fall down, so he can catch her. Until then he is powerless. The therapist sends us home, the treatment is over. Yes, but, my parents say. What now? The therapist says he will send the report to the health insurance. My sister reels across pavement in front of the practice, I go to training.

The frost forms patterns on the car windows. My father has to scrape his car free from ice before he goes to work in the morning. Sometimes he gives me a lift to school. I wear strappy tops under my knitted jumper. If I sit next to the radiator in the classroom I can pull the turtleneck over my head and show my shoulders. It's always warm at Paul's. I go to his after school; he likes my shoulders. I hardly see my sister. When I come home all I do is watch the telephone and wait for it to ring. I watch television, look at the crumbs on the floor, I play with the curtains, I think about Paul, I don't notice shadows. Sometimes my sister wipes round the room. She isn't mad, I think. She gets too high marks for that. But she isn't my sister any more. My sister has gone away, and she won't ever come back, I think. I try to be quiet until I get undressed. I don't want to be noticed. My parents are too exhausted to see.

At night I slip into the gym hall with Paul. I got the key from Perry, to set up before the class. We unfold the trampoline, it's huge. We put it along the big windows, they go from the floor to the ceiling, the gym is on the first floor. We lie down on the trampoline and look up to the sky. Outside are streetlights, their light is too bright. Paul talks about his dog, it's a mongrel. His father took it with him; he doesn't live here any more. They see each other once a month, mostly they play with the dog. I look at Paul while he is speaking. He has a big nose which curves far away from his pointed face. I can't imagine that I will not like Paul some time in the future. I put my hand on his.

Do you want to hear it? I ask. But I know he has fallen asleep. I wrote the sentences in my maths book. I know them off by heart. 'Everything is so slow that nothing passes. Everything seemed to have ended long ago, but it never stops, like the nautilus in the ocean, the ancient snail, we sink, a bundle, clinging to each other. We close our eyes and softly feel for our heartbeat.' I stop and look at Paul. He is translucently pale when he sleeps. He presses his fists into his eyes. I twist his hands round, he wakes up.

Foodstuffs disappear from the kitchen. It takes a while before I notice. I don't notice when the second vanilla pudding disappears from the fridge. My mother hasn't eaten it; my father doesn't like sugary rubbish. My parents don't say anything to me, or to my sister. Then a tub of ice-cream goes missing, a whole litre. Three days later another one goes. My mother buys four new tubs. My parents hold their breath. My mother stuffs the freezer full of litre tubs of vanilla ice-cream. She buys the best, the most expensive brand. Skimmed milk, butter fat, glucose syrup, sugar, colour beta-carotene, bourbon vanilla, flavour enhancer. The ice-cream is a fat accelerator, a sugar bomb, my sister never touches the stuff. The ice-cream disappears. The empty packets pile up in the rubbish bin. No-one says anything. My mother checks the toilet for traces of vomit, under the rim, too. My parents listen when my sister goes to the toilet, but it sounds normal.

After several days I notice something too, although I am never at home. My mother already has seventeen loyalty points from the ice-cream firm. She is afraid and relieved, my father is relieved and afraid. My sister is eating, she shovels the ice-cream down. My sister's belly is sore, but she keeps on eating, even when it hurts. Her stomach has shrunk. I look at my sister. Not long ago she weighed half as much as I do, but every day she puts on weight. She is becoming doughy. She eats a kilo of ice-cream a day on top of breakfast, lunch, dinner. At mealtimes she only manages diet portions. A thin slice of bread with low-fat spread, she can't eat any more. But the ice-cream goes down well, the ice-cream melts and slips and comforts. The slices of bread slowly get thicker. When she eats two slices one morning she only manages half a slice that evening. My sister never eats ice-cream in front of us. She hides herself away to gorge. With every kilo on her ribs the tears flow. My sister cries. She hasn't cried for five years. Now she sobs the whole time. I see her swollen, red eyes. It hurts to look at her. My sister says she doesn't have anything to believe in. She doesn't know up from down. She says she was already dead. She says she is weak, she hates herself. But that's nothing new, that was always the case. I wait. My sister eats. That's all she does. We don't know why.

Two Voices

'The best film in the world?' Lydia said on the phone. 'I've forgotten its name, I can just remember individual scenes. The film started with a wedding; the bride and groom were never in shot. Just a woman in the last pew in the church. Behind her was standing a man with a moustache who had come in late. They were both listening to the priest. They didn't look sad or happy. The ceremony didn't seem to mean that much to them. The man scanned the church as if he were looking for something. The woman in the last pew hadn't noticed the man standing behind her. Without looking around she twisted her hair round at the nape of her neck and pinned it up. Her armpits were carefully shaved.'

I listened to Lydia and picked fluff from the trousers of my suit. Lydia lisped. I bet she had a snub nose and a round, flat face. Bored and noble like a persian cat, that's how I imagined her. Sometimes, without my knowing why, she would suddenly speak very quietly and squeeze the sounds from deep in her throat, as if she were whispering indecencies to me. It irritated me. The lisp and her bright voice made her sound very young. I didn't know how old she was, but my brother reckoned she was in her late twenties.

'Tell me more,' I asked her. 'I can't think of the name of the film either. Is there a murder later? On an ocean yacht?'

Lydia said I was way off the mark, there were no dead people in this film.

From the Indian restaurant below rose the smell of

cumin and cardamom. They brewed chai there round the clock. It was long past midnight. The street outside my window was dark and empty. I reached for the bottle of water.

'The story takes place in Italy, that's very important,' Lydia continued. 'In Italy the sky curves very high – literary critics only understood that very late. Previously they used to try to measure love as if it came from one particular place, it was always at the same latitude. They would enter the number of kisses into a table, that's how they rated passion. They didn't take account of different temperaments. They thought Shakespeare was frigid. But actually it's a question of your standpoint. England just happens to lie where it does, in the Atlantic. The people there are more uptight as a result. However researchers said that sensuality was on ice there.'

'That's nonsense,' I interrupted her. 'Skirts are shorter in England than anywhere else.' I had noticed that on a language holiday ten years ago.

'Yes,' Lydia murmured, 'hemlines go up as the shares go up. Long skirts for falling exchange rates. That makes sense, doesn't it? The stockbrokers look at the catwalk to know what business is going to be like. Funny that mini-skirts stand for an upturn. I thought they acted as a distraction during bad times.'

'That's just a modern superstition,' I said. My father had told me about the skirt rule – this apparently curious connection between fashion and the economy. 'Basically it's the good old "less is more", post-war wisdom.' I had said that last thought out loud inadvertently. Lydia cleared her throat.

'I guess neither of us understands anything about money,' she said conciliatorily. 'Has it come to you yet, what the film is called? You definitely know it. You must know it.'

'I don't remember any Italian wedding where two people meet each other. But I expect that happens in every film from the Mediterranean.'

'Not like in this film it doesn't. The reception after the

ceremony took place in a country manor. The man and the woman went somewhere away from the others. They walked across a broad lawn. It was night-time. Their bodies didn't touch. They were wearing black – a single-breasted suit and a cocktail dress. They didn't talk much, hardly spoke at all. They probably said it was chilly, that they would go home soon. I could tell by their body language. The man's arched eyebrows dropped a little and he seemed to become calmer. The woman was holding a whisky glass; at some point she put it down. She asked for a cigarette; he passed her one and looked for a lighter in his jacket pocket. She spotted that it had fallen through a hole into the lining, she could see the bulge. She didn't say anything.'

I didn't actually know Lydia. That is, I had only known her for a few minutes – my brother had pressed her to my ear and disappeared. He had whispered to me that she liked talking about films. I had once edited the copy for a film book. That was years ago during my apprenticeship at a printer's, shortly before the profession ceased to exist. But everything Lydia said to me was unfamiliar. She didn't seem to notice. She asked questions persistently and there was something insistent in her voice, as if her concern was urgent. Slowing her down excited me. My days had become very long. It was May and I didn't have a job.

'If only I knew what the film was called,' Lydia said. 'It's on the tip of my tongue, but I just can't get it. And yet it was the best film I've ever seen. I often go to the cinema when I'm in cities I don't know. Cinemas are the same everywhere. They're like egg cartons, you can't crack when you're inside them, even when there's a tornado raging on screen. I saw this film in Kiev. The cinemascreen had red velvet seats. There were lots of advertisements before the film and all the slogans were in Ukrainian. The Cyrillic alphabet made me despair: at first glance it appears legible; on a second glance indecipherable. They could be drawing pretzels for all the difference it makes to me. I speak English and a bit of French, but that's it. I can read drinks menus in a few more languages.'

Lydia was an air hostess. My brother had told me that. He knew her through a friend in Baden-Baden who tested cars for Mercedes in Spain. The test track is in the plains south of Madrid. My brother's friend had got to know Lydia in the air over the French plateau. They had often met on the same route and he had ordered orange juice with no ice-cubes every time. On the third flight she had passed him the full plastic beaker without a word. Now I had her at my ear.

'So whassit like in Ukraine then?' I asked.

'I was only there for two days. When I wanted to go to the toilet I had to wait until someone went through the door first. I didn't know the Cyrillic letters for Ladies and Gents. It was winter, there were hardly any street lamps, the ground was sheer ice, nobody gritted. I fell over on a steep street by the cathedral and slipped two metres down the slope. The seat of my trousers was wet, I thought everyone could see it. I bought twenty pirate CDs in the underground stations. There weren't many CD burners back then. There, under the ground, they were playing Falco, 'Rock me Amadeus'. The Dnêpr was as wide as a lake; the current pushed the ice-slabs together to make floating mountains. The houses had tall doors like for giants. Everything was much bigger, at least it seemed like that to me.'

'How did you understand the film? Was it in English?' I asked.

With one eye I watched the numbers changing on the digital display on my CD player. It was like a countdown in reverse, a finite, regular passing of time. At that moment the last sound of track number eight faded out. In ten seconds the display would jump to song nine and would start counting again from zero.

'In Ukraine all films are dubbed,' Lydia replied. 'Into Ukrainian, of course, or Russian. I didn't understand a word. But it was still the best film I had ever seen.'

I don't like going to the cinema, I watch films at home

on video. My brother is the one who likes the cinema. He enjoys going out too. I like my brother, he's funny. Women like that.

'Hello?' Lydia was saying, 'Are you still there?'

I hadn't been listening. I blew air out my nose.

'I asked you something,' she said.

'Yes, I'm here,' I stated stupidly.

'No, before that,' she said impatiently. 'I asked you something before.'

Quickly I responded: 'Excuse me madam – said the hedgehog, and got down from the brush.'

It was one of my worst jokes. Unfortunately I couldn't forget it. Lydia didn't laugh, she was quiet. The telephone connection crackled.

'I don't even know what I'm talking to you for,' she said then.

My mother had said this line to my father hundreds of times. She used to say it on Sundays when he fell asleep in front of the television. She said it when he dismissed her friends' worries with a shrug of the shoulders. We came to hear the phrase almost daily. 'I don't even know what I'm talking to you for.' The words made me sad. There's no way Lydia could guess that, and I wouldn't tell her either.

'Do you know my brother well?' I asked.

'Hm...' She was still sulking. Then she decided to lie: 'I have to go and move my car. Sorry. Good night!'

I could hear she didn't regret anything. 'But you don't have a car,' I said.

'Did your brother tell you that?'

She seemed annoyed. So I was right. Outside the window the crescent moon hung orange behind the rows of houses. It looked like a laughing mouth drawn by a child.

'The man and the woman in the film, where do they go after the reception?' I asked. I wanted to distract Lydia.

'Nowhere! Credits. Music.'

She was clearly pursing her lips tightly, as if toads would

41

spring from her mouth otherwise.

'There's no point recounting the film,' she said after a short pause. 'You'll never understand it anyway.'

'Understand what?'

'Forget it! My parking ticket ran out an hour ago.' She was sticking to the story about the car. I decided to join in. 'Okay, I'll pay the fine. Talk to me. Why are you looking for this film? How did we get onto this?'

She laughed soundlessly. Then she said seriously, 'You remind me of the man. The man who walks across the lawn with the woman.'

I didn't know what to say. I was surprised that I reminded Lydia of someone. She didn't know me, but she had at least seen the man in the film once. 'If you were here,' I said finally, 'I'd offer you wine now.'

'Thanks, I prefer Campari,' she retorted.

I found that affected, and said so.

'Whatever you say.' Her voice was cold. No doubt she was inventing new excuses not to talk with me.

'What did the man look like?' I asked quickly.

'Black and white, the film was in black and white. He had short hair, a moustache. The film was set in the sixties. His suit had a very severe cut. People then mostly wore formal clothing, similar hats, the same haircut.'

I wondered which question I had missed earlier.

It was probably something important, some revelation. While I was thinking about it I very nearly missed what Lydia was saying again.

'The images in the film were long and calm. Sometimes almost nothing happened. They exchanged glances, gestures. The man looked at the woman, the woman looked away. They spoke about insignificant things – at least that was the impression I got – unfortunately I couldn't understand it. The rooms were sparsely furnished. The woman picked up a newspaper, knocked over a plant as she went past, and left the flower lying there. Her behaviour, the scenery, it was all very decorative. It was also sad and empty.'

Lydia was trying to find the right words, and wasn't paying attention to me anymore. What she said sounded vague and clearly had something to do with form and meaning. That went over my head. I imagined Lydia's uniform. Naturally the costume made her nameless and unapproachable, perfect and sexy. Stewardesses are second only to nurses; every man dreams about stewardesses. Lydia suddenly interrupted her flow of speech. She had noticed my thoughts drifting. An unpleasant silence followed.

'I lied,' she said curtly. 'You don't remind me of the man in the film at all.'

'Good, I was starting to worry.' I didn't want to let my disappointment show. 'Filmstars only attract trouble. They are good-looking, have large houses, lots of money and two ex-wives that they pay maintenance to after the divorce. If I resembled this bloke, I'd definitely be sitting behind bars soon.'

'Yeah, who'd want to be a filmstar,' Lydia said mockingly. She suddenly sounded tired. 'It's late now. I have to hang up.'

I didn't answer. No sound came from the receiver. We were both quiet for a long time. I spoke into the silence. 'How about we meet up?' I asked. 'I mean, if you have time and happen to be in the area.'

'What's that supposed to mean? Is that an invitation?'

I was in Passau, in the east on the border with Austria, and she was in Baden-Baden on the western border with France. There was no way she would happen to be passing by.

'We could meet halfway,' I suggested. 'And go for a meal. If you tell me a place I'll be there.'

I wanted to know what she looked like, what she smelled like, how she walked, whether she bared her top teeth when she laughed, whether she was tall or short, pale or dark. Lydia laughed, her laugh sounded happy. I joined in.

'Do you fancy it?' I asked, rhetorically. 'How about a hotel? If we share a room it will be cheaper.' I held my breath.

'I don't really know if that's a good idea,' she said.

'We'll only know afterwards.' I was all ready to start looking through a hotel guide.

But then Lydia said something which cut short all my dreams: 'I'm married.'

So as not to stay silent I asked, 'How long for?'

'Three years. We met on the train. He carried my case.'

'That's nice' was the only thing that came to me. 'I presume he gets very cheap flights?'

She ignored my question.

'Did you have a church wedding?' I asked.

'You're not interested in that.' She was right. I felt caught out.

'You interrupted me,' she pointed out. 'I wasn't finished with the film. I remember another scene. After the wedding the man and the woman didn't see each other. Years passed. They bumped into each other again by chance, at another party. It was a warm day in autumn. The big yellow house with petunias at the windows stood all alone in its own grounds – houses in films always stand alone – on a hill over the river which shimmered golden in the afternoon sun.'

'I thought the film was black and white,' I said.

Apparently she had dragged the telephone into a bare, tiled room, because I could hear an echo when she answered. 'Even so you can still see colours. Don't you?'

'No,' I said. 'If something is in black and white I see black and white, that's all.'

'You've got no imagination. I don't think you would have liked the film. There wasn't much dialogue.'

'Maybe,' I said. 'Normally I'm not fussy. I watch whatever's on, regardless. But there are lots of things that can keep me away from the cinema. Sometimes, on my way there, I hear a bad song on the radio. My mood sinks and I'll turn around.'

'You're funny... As soon as the lights go down there's no radio, no bad mood. You are transported to where the man and woman are, for example. At this second party the woman wasn't on her own. She came accompanied by another man. Presumably the two were living together – they looked intimate. But when she saw the man with the moustache, her old acquaintance, she walked over to him. They talked for a long time and later they went for a walk up the hill. At the top they turned around. They saw something unusual. Below, by the house, a couple arrived. They were just getting out of the car, about fifty yards away from them. It was them. But it might also have been an illusion. The air was shimmering in the heat by now.'

'How did the film end?' I asked.

'The reel started to burn. Something had gone wrong in the projector. Suddenly there were flames on the screen. It looked strange, seeing the celluloid burning, projected in front of us while the real fire was behind us. The screening was stopped. That's probably why I can't forget the film.'

'You could have got it out on video,' I said.

'How? I don't know the name!' I heard her smile. 'I thought you might be able to help me.'

'I don't think I've seen the film. It sounds familiar but that's probably just because of the story.'

'Yes, probably.'

We were silent, both lost in our thoughts. Lydia was the first to speak. 'We could meet anyway. I'm not a slave. What about you?'

It was only now that I noticed the music had stopped ages ago. I pressed the eject button. The silver disc was still spinning as the cover opened. I said nothing.

'I'm in Salzburg on the fourth of June. You could come over.' Lydia gave a hotel name and added, 'Just turn up. If you want.'

'Okay,' I said. 'Sure.' My heart pounded in my throat but my head was empty. Outside it was getting light. The clouds were darker than the sky.

'Think about it and tell your brother... don't tell your brother anything. Tell him not to call any more.' She said goodbye, quick and non-committal. A moment later it was like our conversation had never happened. Except my ear hurt. I had been pressing it too hard against the receiver.

Overgrown

When I turned seventeen I dreamt of Flip's brother, the butcher. I hardly knew him but nevertheless he turned up in my dreams. He said the cotton wool balls had run out and I should dry my tears. I took the sausage skin he held out, crawled out from under the bed and yawned. I wanted to hug some trees, they would comfort me. But the oak trees in the street had been felled a long time ago.

I lay on the embankment and listened for trains. It was a long time before one came along. Our branch line led into the middle of nowhere. The field I was lying on was damp, luscious green. The grass tickled my nose. Snot made its way down my gullet. My voice sounded stuffed up.

It wasn't so long ago that the adviser at the job centre had suggested I give school another try. He said otherwise I wouldn't have many chances in life. I knew about chance from the lottery fairy and her whirling balls. Numbers were read out and my grandparents tried to interpret the rules. They had won some years ago, but had to share the sum with lots of friends because they had filled out the ticket together after a long night in the garden. My grandmother's skirt was crumpled by then and my grandfather, the quiet carpenter, had insisted that his friends choose numbers on the lottery ticket. Their winnings, divided by ten, were only enough for a piss-up. I looked up to my grandfather. His drawn mouth in his furrowed face seemed to snarl at everyone: I don't need dentures, I can bite you without. Watch out!

I said to the man from the job centre that I wasn't interested in chances, that was all humbug. He rummaged in his papers, asked me to be patient and, after looking for a long time, he pulled out an envelope. He printed out a standard letter and licked the fold of the envelope with his fleshy tongue so carefully there might have been drugs in there. While he was doing it I used the time to rip up the brochure for 'new orientations' into precisely thirty little pieces, counting 'love, friendship, hate. Love, friendship, hate' as I did it. I stopped at 'hate'.

For your parents, young lady.

The official obviously didn't feel I was worth addressing as an adult. I took the incendiary letter from his hand and stuck it in the front pocket of my Adidas rucksack. The adviser pressed a button on the side of his desk. Out in the corridor a number flicked round on the display. My number disappeared and another inquisitive young person scuffed their way from the waiting room to this office to get his verdict.

I don't need a school leaving certificate. My boyfriend works on a farm in Australia. I'm going to become a nun. I'll stock vending machines. I've always wanted to do that!

It only briefly crossed my mind to say those things. I didn't see why I should volunteer a single word when they only thought in percentages here anyway. I left without saying goodbye. The adviser let the frog on his screen catch flies again. Every time it caught one the computer celebrated with a trill.

In front of Kaiser's supermarket I saw the chicken man with his stand on wheels. So today was Thursday. Only Friday to go for me and then the relentless weekend begins again. At home my parents moaned in frustration in their air-conditioned silicosis, walkers flooded my places in the village. At the weekend I crawled under the headphones of my

Walkman. But today was Thursday and there was time and place enough to escape. I got myself one of the fatty orange chickens from the rotisserie. I wanted the one at the top, with the unnaturally straight leg. It stuck out, like the chicken had been trying to ice skate. I thought it was touching.

With a bottle of ketchup from the supermarket and the dripping tinfoil pouch on my knee, I perched on the empty stands of the football ground. Not a person in sight. At my back the alsatians belonging to the groundkeeper barked in their kennels. I tore the chicken apart using my hands and teeth, I dipped my tongue into the mound of ketchup at the edge of the pouch and gulped everything down. The only thing I left was the carcass. Then I read the letter. I ripped open the envelope and unfolded the paper with fatty chicken-fingers.

With no School Leaving Certificate... doesn't respond... further addresses...

I didn't need to know any more. I tore the letter into tiny scraps.

I looked up, over the stands. I thought about Flip, the butcher's brother. He often used to lie in the sun by the tennis courts at the back there. I used to saunter past him every Tuesday carrying my tennis racquet. Flip was a walking ribcage with fuzz on his top lip. On his head he had bleached orangey-blond hair with dark roots. Since he had turned fourteen, four years ago, he had worn army shirts, two in rotation – at least I hoped so. He was nearly two heads taller than me. I was at eye level with the brown frizz that crept out of his cut-off sleeves in the summer. In the morning he went to the abattoir, for the rest of the day he counted sausages. In the evening he looked after the party delivery service. We had both been in the tennis club together. Flip had given up. He smoked. Dried banana skins, flour, crumbled pencil leads, cactus leaves, hair. He had tried everything already. He was looking for a cheap hit, but in vain. He had recently acquired a dealer, everyone knew that. He got Afghan Black delivered now. The Afghan was stuck into the motors of cars which crossed at Gibraltar for him. Flip acted like even the grower in Morocco thought of him, the brave toker, in wonder. Flip spoke about the Spanish smugglers like they were on first name terms. He had never met them. In his imagination Flip travelled with the Afghan Black the whole way. In reality he didn't even have a passport. He had never needed one. But I only found that out when I got closer to him. I had never had much to do with him in the tennis club. A few times he swept the court before my training session. I watched him doing it and was annoyed at how slowly he went, that was all. Flip left the club, never wore sports gear again, and from one day to the next he started to smell of adventure. He sat in front of Kaiser's and grinned at me. I wasn't sure how to react. One look from me could shatter glass. My mirror had told me that at an early age. I could freeze mothers to the spot by staring at their babies like their nose had fallen off. Flip wasn't scared, he was probably too stoned. But he saw the crocodile on my left breast and the white tennis socks on my milk-white calves. I put my arm across the crocodile and casually turned the collar of my polo shirt up. Flip pointed to the bag in my hand. I showed him the chocolate Easter bunny and the Angel Delight for my lunch.

Special offer, right? Easter was ages ago.

Flip rolled his r's like he'd spent a thousand years in Siberia. I asked if he was originally from Russia – he sounded like it. It was supposed to be a joke. I hadn't expected to be let into family secrets.

My real father is a Russian. My brother, the butcher, the old man we live with is his dad, not mine though. I only call him 'Papa' to be considerate. My mother met the Russian who became my father at a trade fair. Nothing's been going on between her and the old man for a long time. She conceived me at the butchers' fair.

Backing up the story was the fact that the brothers, the butcher and Flip, were about as alike as a cuckoo and a donkey. I didn't know what to say to that. My parents worked for the child protection agency and had known each other since uni. I walked on. The shopping bag banged against my thighs.

No-one was home. I whipped the Angel Delight I had just bought with the hand-held whisk and thought about Flip. On the couch I stuffed myself with the foamy mass of pudding. I had shut the blinds in the living room so the light didn't reflect on the television screen. I watched the young Aborigine hunting in the outback, with no cover. He ran barefoot, agile and soundless like the wind, taking huge strides right up to the little kangaroo. It didn't seem to notice him. But suddenly it turned its head and looked straight at the hunter. He froze immediately, his right foot up in the air, his spear seemed to be carved into his outstretched hand. He stood so completely still he could have been a ghost. The kangaroo went back to grazing. A second later it was dead. The spear had hit the carotid artery cleanly. The aborigine disembowelled the animal and carried the butchered limbs on his belt through the heat. Blood and bodily fluids mingled on his skin. Every afternoon I used to watch the schools' programmes about foreign tribes and animals. I picked at my spots and dreamt of malaria, moustaches under tropical headgear, and the precariousness of hammocks.

In the evening I went to the youth centre. The table football was occupied. Two lads had been playing for two hours. They wouldn't let anyone else on. I banged on the edge of the table and demanded. Their reaction came promptly: where's your partner? You can't play on your own. Then there's no one to defend. Clear off.

I toddled off. A bald head threw a dart directly in front of my nose. It was very nearly an accident. I drew my breath but the bloke had already shoved me to one side. I rubbed my funny bone.

The back third of the hall was in semi-darkness. There

were a few old sofas from a skip and an old-fashioned table and chairs with cut-out hearts in the seat backs and a corner bench. Two kneecaps in military trousers stuck up next to the table-top. I approached hopefully. I had guessed right. Flip had arranged himself along the corner bench and was meditating. A bit of fuzzy belly flashed between shirt and trousers. His belly-button was a semi-circular knob. I quite fancied pushing it in, but instead I kicked and punched the Coke machine next to the group sitting down and nicked a bottle which I took and sat down next to Flips. I acted nonchalant.

The lid will blow soon for sure. They're all still camping out in the German embassies in Prague and Budapest. Have you heard anything? I mean, your father's Russian.

My father doesn't even pay maintenance.

But your mum's bloke pays for you, doesn't he? And you live there.

Flip snorted. He asked if I was from social services.

That's how it started.

We drove the butcher's car to the river Rhein. Flip had lost his driving licence and I was only sixteen. His brother didn't know he had the car. Flip held the steering wheel with one hand. His free hand rested on his upper thigh. He got out at the river bank and pissed in the river. I watched him, hunched over in a shiny baseball jacket, through the windscreen. The floodlights from the sports ground on the other side of the river were reflected in the waves which slapped against the bank. Suddenly the light on the ground went out. I could hear the rats under the stones on the embankment. Flip wandered back to the car. His shoelaces were undone. He had to crawl over me to get back in the car because the driver's door wouldn't open. He trod in my groin. We sat there in silence, stared at the water. He turned the radio on, '... F-R-E-I-H-E-I-T, F-R-E-I-H-E-I-T...' Marius Müller-Westernhagen's 'Freedom', the anthem of the autumn. I thought, the battery will go dead, the engine won't start, we'll be stuck here, my parents will hit the roof, the Rhein will flood. I said nothing.

All that came to me as I threw the chicken bones away. The tinfoil pouch wouldn't fit in the green bin on the sports ground. It threatened to fall out. I walked away quickly. I thought about Flip's teeth, which looked like they had been nibbled away by mice, and his lopsided smile. I missed it.
You talk to the drunks, you eat bad food for the waiter's sake. You're too nice, Flip had once told me.

I had grabbed him under his arms, but my tickling turned into scratching. He let the accusation drop. We were standing behind the marquee at the football club, next to the sports ground. Inside strikers and defenders snorted into the puddles of beer on the tables. The band was playing a German song to the tune of the Wild Rover. Everyone bawled along. We were standing in the entrance. We cast huge shadows on the wall of the marquee behind the stage. We felt fantastic, we were outside, we didn't belong. The footballers didn't even notice us staring them to bits. The crocodiles on my chest had long since swum downstream. I was wearing one of my new batik shirts. The dye had ruined the white sheets that my mother washed after my dyeing attempt. Everything turned red.

Behind the marquee Flip pushed my T-shirt up and lifted me onto the bonnet of a car. I wrapped my legs around him. I could smell a dash of Bonnie & Clyde in his hair. The groundskeeper's alsatians bayed. As Flip and I were gasping in unison Flip's cousin, skinny Karla, came round the corner. She had been collecting beer bottles for the deposit, enough for fags. Flip let me drop to the ground. I straightened my T-shirt. Karla acted like we'd only been eating ice-cream and started burbling immediately.

This dead-end town is worse than the desert... footballer's do... hah! Don't make me laugh... do you know this one?

How many social workers does it take to change a lightbulb?

Karla seemed to save the jokes from the freebie newspapers.

Shall we go to mine? Flip suggested.

Five.

That was Karla. But no one wanted to know any more. She shut up, offended.

There was never anything to eat at Flip's other than noodles and muesli bars. He had put his parents' old leather suite down in the cellar. Karla and I sprawled on it. Flip tried to make coffee. It was ten at night. The coffee tasted of vinegar. Flip's mother had tried to de-scale the machine and it still had traces of vinegar. We drank cognac from the living room cabinet and topped up the bottle with apple juice. The old butcher and his wife were in the marquee, Flip's brother was doing a stock take and we were undisturbed. Karla had moles, as many as a dalmatiaon has spots. I teased her about them. She was three years older than me and worked in the offices of the sugar factory. Now it was late summer, the tractors with their trailers of sugar beet drove through the village every day again.

Karla claimed that every now and then a beet would fall onto the road and people would die in the accidents this caused. 'We thank Southern Sugar for their generous support for the funeral' supposedly stood at the bottom of the obituaries. Karla told us that she used to sign the orders for the wreaths. 'With sympathy' she would write on the condolences cards. 'We will endeavour to ensure that in future none of our sugar beet can come loose and endanger traffic.' Of course no one actually did anything about it. In reality the firm apparently even factored in the possibility that every hundred thousandth lump of crystal sugar might contain arsenic. The firm's insurance premium absorbed this risk. Karla was on her third glass of cognac already.

My lips were burning, the alcohol was turning my

stomach into a ball of fire. I had only ever drunk bubbly at
Christmas before. Flip spread tobacco onto the cigarette
paper. It was his sacred ritual. I flung my arms around his
neck and stuck myself to his back. The leather sofa made
farting sounds as Karla slid away from us. Flip and me were
the couple you put coins in a slot for, greedily gazing at the
porn-stage. A thousand eyes admiring us from behind
embrasures wouldn't have been enough to satisfy me. I was
sure we were the best. Anyone who saw us had to agree. For
Karla I ran my tongue up Flip's neck. See, every one of my
movements said, see how good we have it, see what we can
do? Flip was smoking with his eyes half closed. He didn't
seem to notice me, but Karla did. I fingered his trousers,
keeping my eyes on Karla. She reached for the remote
control. Crime Scene flickered black and white from the oak
veneer set. Schimanski was frying an egg. It went wrong. He
threw it away and drank a raw egg from a glass instead. Karla
watched like they were showing recipes and she was
starving.

It was a long time since I'd gone down to Flip's cellar after
school. I grew tired just thinking about it. I had to sit down.
The stone spheres that spouted water in the fountain had
been turned off for the winter now. Exhausted, I flopped
down on top of the biggest sphere. I counted the clinker
bricks in the façade of the building society. The digital clock
on the southern side of the building showed fourteen minutes
to two. The schoolkids should be coming soon. The first lot
with their pointy faces would whizz past the market square
on their pedal bikes, the next wave would stream out of the
bus in a lazily pulsating mass; neck scarves and sweatbands in
neon colours leaping out. I was hungry, even though a whole
bird was pushing its way through my intestines. I thought
about Flip's liplines, the shaved bloody edges of his mouth.
His face had changed all of a sudden after the evening of the
footballers' do. He didn't want to play peepshow any more.

He was angry with me and I didn't know why.

He said, nothing! Nothing's up. Why should there be? I need to think about things. I have problems. The world doesn't know who I am. Am I really meant to count sausages until I'm old and done? I ought to have played football in the Bundesliga, but my parents sent me to tennis club.

I wanted to give him running spikes then, I wanted to force the world to see him. I would have named a parade after him. I would have done all that. But it wasn't what was needed, he didn't want it. I started to picture the reason why.

In my head the same images kept on trickling. Flip and Karla, with tongue sausage in between them, like one fresh from the mincing machine, their jaws grinding meticulously, the mouths devouring each other, smacking their lips. I had never seen it. I had only dreamt it.

While I twirled my curls, painting myself new mouths every hour, mouths which prayed 'Flip', I saw Flip and Karla behind me in the bathroom mirror, a plait braided together, the two of them. Their braiding unwound languidly, showed me breasts, with brown moles, and Flip's fingertips, which bored and pressed, tipped, legs in the other's step, waves in their hips. When I turned round they were gone, disappeared into the depths of the mirror.

I said to Flip, there's something going on between the two of you. Just admit it. If you admit it I can forgive you.

I have nothing to confess.

Be honest for once. Once. Try it, it's really easy. Okay, I'll go first, then you. A story, a short story. Something we haven't told each other. A dirty truth.

Are you looking for a fight?

Trust is what I'm looking for. You didn't go to Sunday School, how are you supposed to know what that is? Maybe you have a sense though: trust is what the slogans in the adverts bestow. Trust is what has made the jolly green giant so big.

You can spare the nonsense. I know what you look like when you come. That's enough for me.

I took a deep breath. I took your fountain pen. The gold one, that you looked for like mad two weeks ago. It didn't fall out in the cinema. I've got it. Your turn now. Tell the truth!

He didn't want to. He wrinkled his nose in anger about the pen, and his eyes darkened. I wouldn't let it lie. I pressed the truth point on his collarbone and he started: it's easy. You open your eyes wide whenever we kiss. You stare at me like I'm the dentist. But I can't help you either. After school you eat my noodles and muesli bars. You never buy anything. You stink. You smell of old fish. I hate the sea. More?

You just happened to be there. You could have been anyone else. It wouldn't have made any difference to me. But then you puffed yourself up with my dreams, stuffed yourself with my desires, which you would fulfil, and I just came along for the ride. You can't do this to me now...You can't say I didn't want it.

And he took it back. Like an empty bottle at the depot, he took everything back. He exchanged the words for his lopsided smile. I didn't need to pay a deposit any more. He had already cashed it in.

I saw Karla at the pigeon lofts. I had dumped Flip after our conversation. The sand in front of the cages was freshly raked. Clean, even lines criss-crossed the paths in front of the cages. Everything was tidy; it was open day. Karla walked up and down in between the cages. Half of the village was there to admire the pigeons. Pigeons that could no longer walk because their feet feathers were too long. Pigeons that could no longer eat by themselves because their beaks have a wattle that means they can only be fed liquids through a tube. Pigeons that have had abscesses since birth but are kept for their particularly pretty eye colour. The pigeons cooed like they were trying to conjure something up.

Karla poked a straw at a pigeon which was once supposed to be a carrier pigeon. The pigeon picked at anything that came near it. I noticed that Karla turned her feet in when she walked. She had pigeon feet. She continually threatened to fall over her own toes. I was pleased about that. I started speaking to her. She didn't seem surprised. It was like she had been expecting me. I began with the birds: so are you wanting to get into the pigeon business? Is the mail too expensive for you? How far do you think they can find their way?

Karla answered the questions I'd just thrown out there quite seriously: there was one in America once which flew nearly four thousand kilometres back home. That's just mad.

I don't think so. Pigeons can see more than we can. They can see the earth's magnetic field, polarised sunlight, ultraviolet patterns of light in the sky. Ever heard of that? And they can smell. They follow scents.

What about you?

I get people to drive me, take me around in the car. I can't read maps anyway.

There was something funny in that. But Karla was probably only laughing because laughing was what Karla could articulate best. She always laughed when she couldn't think of anything else. I hoped that there were evil cells hiding under one of her hundreds of bloody moles waiting to go black and multiply and in the end they would kill Karla's laugh too. Like a good girl I regretted it immediately.

I forced Flip to do it standing up, because I wanted to be sure that I wasn't lying in another girl's sweat. He found it tiring. I noticed how he would concentrate on something far behind me in order to come. He forced a smile, I parried with a babbling that ran senselessly through his ears, with no beginning and no end, like glue. Flip shoved Jamiroquai on the ghetto blaster, Emergency on Planet Earth. That was the last I heard from him. He didn't call any more. His mother didn't know where he was. I carved a long red line on my underarm with the nail on my index finger. It looked like blood poisoning.

Once I called the butcher's. I asked for the party delivery service. When I heard Flip's voice I hung up. He sounded cheerful, awake. I didn't know him like that. Karla's moles must have leapt onto him like fleas, bitten his fur, woken him up.

Over, over, over! I yelled into the beeping telephone. I broke up with you yesterday you idiot. You just didn't know it.

But I didn't break us up. We went our separate ways. It passed like a cold, imperceptibly, hesitantly. I never saw them together, I only dreamed them, Flip and Karla. But that was harder to cope with. When you're dreaming you can't shut your eyes.

The paint has run. I won't pay a cent for that, said Frau Meinhardt, to whom the job centre had sent me. Temporary workers, they called daily labourers like me. Frau Meinhardt let me go. My brushstrokes had left sad tears on the door. I understood that no one liked it.

I huddled on the railway embankment and waited for the goods trains with their wagons full of rubble and ironwork. Time passed more quickly when a train rushed past me. I thought about Flip and played with the sausage skin in my hand. If I stretched it to breaking point and held it close to my cornea I could make out something that must have been a mole once. I spat.

Poor Knights

We still talk about her sometimes. We ask ourselves, how do we think she is doing now? We say it distractedly between thoughts of shopping and theatre tickets. We don't really want to know how she is. We think of the Poor Knights that she used to cook: french toast soaked in egg, fried in a pan, gleaming with fat, sprinkled with sugar and cinnamon. The cinnamon was a cold fire, it burnt on the tongue. Poor Knights. We liked it because of the name. We didn't like her name. Gudrun – that's what heroines are called. But she was rather timid.

When we talk about her, we look at our hands. We wiggle our fingers, just to watch the bones play under the lattice of veins. We clasp our hands and listen to the music from the living room. The melody is simple. Just a few notes on a guitar with a regular drumbeat over the top. Calming. We don't listen to anything else. The cups sitting on the low rattan table in front of us have brown tidemarks of tea. We don't bother to rinse them.

Everything has disappeared, Gudrun's dog posters, the embroidered Indian cushions with mirrored amulets, the clothes stand draped with flea market clothes. It seemed impossible to imagine the flat without her in the lounge chair, at the kitchen table, in the window seat, on the velvet sofa, but it has become our place. Gudrun is gone. We remember her perfume best. It used to hang around her like an old curtain when she stepped out of the bathroom. A curtain stored in a damp outhouse. It smelled repulsive, but we still wanted to put our hands in her hair to find out where the smell was coming from. It probably wasn't a perfume at all, but the smell of silk towels mixed with cocoa shampoo and cigarette smoke. We never saw a bottle with a designer name on, or an atomiser that she directed at her neck every morning. Her smell must have been the sum of the things that surrounded her daily. The things that were old, fusty.

The first time we came into Gudrun's flat our cheeks were red from the November wind, our fingers numb inside our gloves. We had written to her, telling her that we wanted to come, that we liked the city, that we were looking for a flat. We could hardly remember her. She had been a disembodied voice on the telephone that called at New Year and on our birthday, interrupted by the clunk of coins in the telephone booth. She didn't have a telephone. They told us she had last been to the village for our christening. We could understand that. It was eight weeks before we got a reply to our letter. Her writing was in tight lines, the letters huddled together, straight up and down. Her handwriting marched. She wrote: 'If you turn the corner by the smoky pub, at midday this month, earlier during the rest of the year, you'll see a street made of gold. The sun shines at you like it's suspended just above the tarmac, like a floodlight set too bright.' We thought it sounded like a kitschy leaflet, like a plump landlady trying to be poetic. We set off at the specified time.

The house proudly displayed a lion's paw on the front door and a glass roof over the stairwell, but the metal on the door was oxidised green and the plaster was falling off the walls. We surveyed the height of the ceilings as we climbed the stairs. The flats had lower ceilings than expected, but on the other hand we thought they seemed warm, easy to heat. We read the names on the doorbells. None of the nameplates were printed, the tenants had all used fountain pen or pencil. On every landing the smell of different foods enveloped us. Red cabbage on the ground floor, pork goulash with bananas on the first, and on the second it was coffee and walnut cake. We sniffed in vain outside Gudrun's door on the third floor. She never cooked. We didn't know that yet. She turned the oven on later, just for us. Her yoghurt grew in a glass in the kitchen, the milk for it was unpasteurised, the cow smell that came off it was enough to turn our stomachs. But we didn't know that yet. We were looking for a place, not food. We shuffled our feet in front of the odourless door, in two minds. We looked out the landing skylight, to see if we could get a look at the flat windows. If there had been net curtains we would have turned and gone.

That's what we had left behind. A lime tree – bare, admittedly – but with a thick trunk and branches directly in our line of sight, blocked the view of the windows.

Who's there? Gudrun yelled in answer to our knocking. We called our names and heard rustling behind the door. Paper was being moved to the side. While that was happening we heard the hummed melody of 'A Ship Will Come'. We knew the words. Our father had kept the record. Whenever we used to leave the sleeve lying around he would pick it up and look at the black and white face with the sweeping eyelashes. When he felt us looking at him he would put it down as if he'd mistaken the sleeve for something else and disappear into the next room. Without speaking. There was nothing he feared more than ridicule. Gudrun was his sister. On that November day five years ago she opened the door to us. Curious, we peered around the hall and into the rooms going off it. There were piles of newspaper everywhere, neatly stacked, in the middle of the room or along the skirting board. They spilled out of cupboards and shelves. Later we discovered the rest of Gudrun's collections too. There was a drawer filled to bursting with rubber bands, one with string, every possible length, some bits were only five centimetres long. Gudrun kept smoothed-out tinfoil in a chest, and stuffed cartons and other packaging into many more boxes. She hoarded so much rubbish it was impossible to ever reuse it all. Souvenirs covered every available surface in the flat. A string of turquoise prayer beads from Iran, a banknote from Odessa printed with a Tartar, a clicking metal bird from India, a wooden giraffe from Africa. Our father had told us that Gudrun was once married to a composer. He had died a long time ago. There was no music in her flat. Sometimes she started to hum, but if we asked her about it she denied ever having made a sound. She wasn't aware she was humming.

We were still standing in the hallway. Gudrun saw us for the first time. She blinked, confused. We were used to that from other people. It would take a while for her to be able to tell one of us from the other. We had exploited that when we were younger. In sports lessons, only one of us had vaulted the horse, and only one of us worked out the physics experiments. We could choose. Gudrun asked our names. We didn't think names would help. She couldn't possibly know which one of us she was addressing at any given moment. She probably avoided the question about our distinguishing features from a false sense of pride. She turned away. Slowly, as if she could only detach herself with difficulty from what was behind her. As soon as she had turned her back on us her movements became hectic. She hurried through the flat, left us standing in the hallway, offered us nuts, but then couldn't find the tin. We dragged our suitcases into a room. It was filled with shelves up to the ceiling, with a mattress lying on the floor. Gudrun followed us. Without challenging our selection she walked out of the room. She murmured something incomprehensible. Finally she shoved the mattress into the middle of the room with her feet. Water course, she said in justification. We told her that we had slept very well even right next to a building site.

It's an internal noise. You can't compare the disturbance from water flowing underground with that from machines. Gudrun had barely left the room before we pushed the mattress back against the wall. Today it seems to us that that was the signal. This place was ours.

The rules were simple. Be quiet and eat. Our father had given us that as a parting gift. He considered this rule to be the guest's duty. In the beginning we kept to it. We lay in bed, we were quiet, we ate. Gudrun only put the heating on when there was frost on the ground. She thought it wasn't necessary yet. When we opened the windows dustballs would fly around in the wind towards our mattress. We blew them away from under the covers. Next to our black sheets, on the brown, dirt-encrusted floorboards, lay the newspapers with the lettings pages. We had thickly circled individual ads, underlined in red, drawn a border round the edges. Our symbols were scribbled so quickly we couldn't decipher them ourselves any more. We guessed at their meaning. Left a message, called back, too expensive, too far away, too small, no bath, no light, too much traffic. We made the calls from a phone booth in the station. The noise around us seemed to come in constant waves. Newspaper vendors called their wares, travellers dragged their suitcases past, loud announcements rang out, trains departed, arrived. None of the landlords offered to show us round, we rang anyway. We wrote to our father: 'Everything fine. You know. We're looking, we'll find. The platforms in the underground are licked so clean, it frightens us. The passengers stand at intervals like a military patrol. Instead of shaking hands, here they look you up and down, from the make of your hat to the soles of your feet. We walk a lot, we get lost. Let's not talk about accommodation. There isn't any here. We go to the department stores instead. Our room here is nice. Light, airy. We would never have believed Gudrun was your sister. Look after yourself.' We signed one on top of the other as usual. Our father was familiar with this knot of letters. He was the only one who would know which of us had written the letter. We had thought of everything. He didn't need to know about our plan.

We went into the kitchen. Gudrun was sitting there. It was dark. A bus drove past in the street outside. The roof of the vehicle reflected the light from the streetlamps into the kitchen. Like a ball of lightning the bright patch wandered across the ceiling. We sat down. Gudrun had a textbook in front of her, Slovenian. She received the packages with the lessons in big yellow envelopes through the post. A grid on a page of a newspaper had advertised thirty-two different courses. From 'sewing from patterns' to 'physics', you can learn everything by packages. It was far too dark to read in the room. Gudrun was staring ahead. We reached for the pretzels in the bread basket, we crunched into the crust. The salt crystals made our lips pucker. Gudrun's voice sounded confidential. I don't even know what the Slovenian language sounds like, she said. We didn't know either. Instead we asked her what the flat's floor-space was. She reckoned 700 square feet. In our head we calculated what the utility bills would cost. Gudrun carried on talking about her language course. The country is so small, it's not very densely populated, but there are fifty different dialects and two possible official forms of pronunciation. That's like there being two types of Queen's English. One of these forms of pronunciation distinguishes between long and short, stressed and unstressed, front and back vowels. In the other one it doesn't matter, there is no difference, no stress. That's the choice that you have. What on earth does it sound like? We didn't reply. The plaster next to the poster of the Nuremberg Rail Museum had opened up. Fine hairline cracks ran the length of the wall between the semi-circular holes, which looked like a chain of white mice biting each other's tails. They were growing in number. We suspected that Gudrun couldn't resist the disintegrating layer of wall and secretly expanded the cracks. Maybe that was her way of passing the time. I don't have a cassette recorder, she said. I can't stand them, those babbling machines. They always send cassettes too, for the course. I pay for them even though I can't listen to them. Suddenly she changed the topic. Have you written to your father? She had seen the letter addressed to him in the hall. Her question was just the preamble to an anecdote we already knew. He ate coal when he was a child, your father. Mother took him to the doctor. She should just let him, he said. Children know what they need. Your father carried on eating coal. He went completely black round the mouth. Luckily for him his milk teeth fell out later on. She laughed. We had started to take food out of the cupboards, acting absent-minded. Gudrun realised. Are you looking for something in particular? I don't have anything in. Do you want something to eat? She took a packet of crispbread out of the washing cupboard. We nodded, but carried on emptying the shelves while she started to whisk the eggs, in order to dip the bread in the slimy mass. While Gudrun was beating the egg with a fork, we piled up around her the packets of potato starch opened years ago, half cubes of stock, bags with lumpy sugar in them. We divided up the leftovers in her kitchen. We threw the foodstuffs that had gone off into a black bag, and put the rest away again. Things ended up in different cupboards. It was more practical that way. Gudrun was lost in preparing the Poor Knights. She didn't seem to notice us. As she was tossing the slices of bread into the pan with sizzling fat, we were just closing the kitchen door behind us. We threw the black bag into the rubbish bin in the yard. When we returned the kitchen was empty. The only things there were two plates with piping hot Poor Knights standing on the table.

Be quiet and eat. That had been our father's advice. We stuck to it. We used it to our advantage. We ate, we said nothing.

Gudrun's supplies were almost used up. It had turned to winter. We stayed in the flat more often. We had learnt how to turn on the blue flickering flames of the gas radiators. Idle and tired from the warmth of the heating we lay on our mattress and listened out for Gudrun, her noises. We waited until she hid away in a room and then we got up. We removed a drawing pin from the flower poster in the toilet. A corner curled up. We were careful. We waited a few days before taking another drawing pin out of the wall, leaving the poster hanging askew. When it fell on the floor we took it away. The marbles on the window sill, which already had thick curls of dust, disappeared one by one. Eventually we lugged the newspapers out in baskets. We gave up on reticence. Gudrun asked after the pile of FAZs behind the door, we said we hadn't seen it. She let the matter drop. We carried on clearing things. Gudrun was increasingly murmuring bits of Slovenian around us. We didn't understand a word. She didn't cook for us any more. The day that we carried the bed frame, solid as prison bars, into our room, Gudrun suddenly appeared in the door. She said: I want you to go. She looked at us, we showed no reaction. She left the house. When she came back, we had changed the locks.

We let Gudrun into the flat, of course. She stood outside the door like we had once done, with a hectic red flush in her cheeks. She didn't say anything. She went into the kitchen, rummaged in the cupboards. The tools she was looking for, presumably a screwdriver or pliers, were nowhere to be found. Her movements were agitated. She didn't look at us. We had thought everything through. She could have shouted at us, threatened us, reported us. But nothing happened. She tried to counter us with silent resistance. With no house key she didn't dare go out any more. She probably feared being made homeless, locked out for ever. She couldn't trust us any more. The only thing she had left was the room keys. We hadn't thought of that. She locked all the doors in the flat.

Only the door to our room stayed open. We had wedged the door open. We didn't lock the door to the flat. We had hoarded supplies. It couldn't take long. We passed the time by reading. 'The gargoyles on the vertices of the roof of the cathedral Notre Dame de Paris rest their thoughtful monkey-faces in their hands, surveying the city with tongues hanging out, sporting horns and wings and the naked torsos of handsome men.' We put the book to one side, we could see the Seine flowing around the island with the church, smell the pondweed which lay along the river banks, hear the seagulls. We would pull out a book from the boxes in front of the bookstands, and note with surprise the German title. We would open the green cloth-bound book and read, 'The gargoyles on the vertices of the roof of the cathedral Notre Dame de Paris rest their thoughtful monkey-faces in their hands, surveying the city with tongues hanging out, sporting horns and wings and the naked torsos of handsome men.' We had fallen asleep.

When we woke up, we had a white crust around the mouth, sleep in our eyes. We scooped water onto our faces in the bathroom. The water was cold, it came out of the tap in annoying spurts, splashed our trousers. Still bleary with sleep we folded the doors of the wardrobe in so we could see our face reflected to infinity. Our twin faces, which were so identical we could fool strangers. In front of the hall of mirrors formed by folding back the doors we pulled faces, gurned, twitched our nose, ears, mouth. Thousands of faces danced in the depths of the mirror. We laughed, we nodded at ourselves. The blind patches on the mirrors bothered us. We would get rid of them. It was only at this point that we noticed the silence. No noises, no groaning in the heating, no sounds of water, no creaking from her rattan chair. We walked through the flat. Hall, kitchen, bedroom, study. The doors were all locked. Gudrun wasn't there.

We waited. Who could she fetch? The police, the neighbours? We were part of the family. A small dismissive wave of the hands in front of our face, behind Gudrun's back, a meaningful glance, that's all it would take. We would be alone again. But the reinforcements didn't come. No-one knocked. Days elapsed. Gudrun didn't come back. We rattled the door-handles, debated whether to break open the locked doors. We left it. The bathroom was open, the water still flowed. We ate vacuum-packed pumpernickel with jam, slurped Japanese packet soup which we made up with hot water from the tap, and drank effervescent vitamin tablets. In the stairwell we breathed in the smells from the neighbours' dinners. One of us always stood at the front door. We didn't go more than one floor away. The days got shorter. We slept a lot. A cold wind blew through the hallway. We had opened the window in our room. We suspected Gudrun had locked herself in one of the rooms. We listened carefully. Nothing, no sounds. We watched the doors. None of them opened. Gudrun was still nowhere to be seen. We wanted to get duplicate keys, a picklock. We were just about to go out to get one when there was a knock. Through the spyhole we saw our father standing outside the door. He looked small and stocky. That was the effect of the fish-eye.

Our father had with him the keys for the locked rooms. We opened the kitchen door. He didn't know which key it was. He had never been in the flat before. We sat down at the kitchen table. He gave us biscuits, crumbly ones with oats stuck in honey. It was a token. Gudrun has... He went quiet. She says there was a big misunderstanding between you and her? The chains of mice formed by the cracks in the wall had grown in length. We studied them thoughtfully while our father was speaking. She has been living here for thirty years, the flat belongs to her. You want to look for a place of your own don't you? He had lit himself a cigarette. The smoke drifted in our direction. We gestured to the ashtray. You changed the locks? Was that necessary? We nodded. Have you swallowed your tongues? A few years ago we would have stuck them out at him. Now we just pressed them against the inside of our front teeth. Our father drummed his forefinger on the table. Then we said, we had moved out, grown up, we were over the hills and far away. He wasn't to interfere. Not any more. He looked at us for a long time, first disbelieving, then determined. He put the room keys down on the table. Kitchen, living room, bedroom. He read the labels on the keyring. He said, you have till Thursday: I want you to put the door key through the letterbox downstairs. Gudrun will come and collect it. If you have a spark of decency left in you then you'll know what you need to do. I hope I'm not mistaken about you. I know you better than any other person. He spared us the story of blood and inheritance. He had a bit of shaving foam on his ear. One of us wetted a finger and dabbed the white from his skin. He turned his head to one side, away from us. After that no one spoke a word. It was the last time we saw each other.

It was all so easy that sometimes it seems incredible. We didn't put the key in the letterbox, instead we bought new furniture, polished the old table top, put flowers in the windows. We avoided the neighbours' questions. A van picked up Gudrun's effects. The removal men told us that Gudrun still lived in the same city, in an apartment on the edge of an industrial estate. When we look out of the window towards the power station we think of her. She never came by. We still talk about her sometimes. We ask ourselves, how do we think she is doing now? We say it distractedly between thoughts of shopping and theatre tickets. We don't really want to know how she is. We are doing fine.

Sleep

My mother came to say goodbye. It wasn't the first time that she was to disappear for some time. She ran her forefinger under her eyes to stop her mascara smearing. Her fingernails were varnished pale blue. My mother had brought me to my grandmother's. I was to stay here a while. She said she had to go for treatment. When she was better she would come and visit me, then soon we could go home again. I didn't know how long a while was. My mother said it all depended how the illness developed. I asked, what's wrong with you? She said it was hard to explain. The illness was in her head.

I had to change school. Before, I lived with my mother in the city, in the lowlands. My grandmother lived in a village in a low mountain range. The mountains were not high, but the roads went up steeply. I found it tiring walking up them. All the important things, school, the shops, the railway factory, were down in the valley. My grandmother's house clung to the mountainside. The vegetables in the garden nearly fell out of the ground. Chunks of rock, some of them as big as your fist, covered in clay, that's what the earth was made of here. When the rain came it washed the stones free. The clay flowed away.

The hills were a slate mountain range, the rock looked like dark grey, slivering brittle. The slate protruded through the earth all over the place, or hung in sharp jags above the road, secured by nets. Beware falling rocks. I soon recognised the road sign. The houses were all studded with the grey slabs. Thus armour-plated, the walls and roofs seemed to repel watchful eyes. On the other side of the valley, on a different range of hills covered in fir trees, a rock as high as a house jutted up out of the bedrock. The rock looked like a scale model of an alpine peak. The escarpments were formed from many thick layers of stone forced together and on the summit there was a cross. I imagined that Abraham was meant to kill his son here; the rock seemed to me to be made for that purpose. 'Take now thy son thine only son Isaac, whom thou lovest, and offer him for a burnt offering,' God had commanded. Abraham had taken fire and knife in his hand when the angel of the Lord called down, 'Lay not thine hand upon the lad.' God had put Abraham to the test. I knew the Bible stories didn't take place in the mountains where my grandmother lived. In reality the rock had been a druid stone. Centuries ago sorcerers had invoked the protection of the sky here. Later Christians erected the iron cross. The many free churches in the area had hoped this would banish the old gods.

My grandmother only had my mother, my mother only had me. My father had gone back to the Czech Republic. I didn't know him. My grandmother hardly spoke about her daughter, my mother. Even on my earlier visits she had only ever asked when my mother would come and pick me up again. But generally she refrained from this question too, for my mother didn't keep to arrangements. Sometimes she said Thursday and only picked me up on Saturday.

This time it took my mother four weeks to get in touch. My grandmother motioned to me to come to the phone. My favourite series was on the television. It was set in the future. A few humans ruled over the rest of the population by encasing themselves in machines that looked like large silver spiders. The subjugated humans thought it was aliens watching over them. When my mother phoned, one of the spiders had just got the hero of the series in its sights and was threatening to destroy him. I wanted to get back to the television quickly. I tried to listen to the dialogue with one ear, and pressed the telephone receiver to my other ear. My mother's voice said she hadn't been allowed to phone, those were the regulations in the clinic. I asked when she would come back. My mother thought it would take her some time to get well again. I wanted to know what was up with her. My mother considered this out loud. She couldn't say her heart, that wasn't quite true. She didn't have any pain. It was like she was numb, she didn't feel anything. I asked if the illness felt like your whole body had fallen asleep. By that I meant the numb feeling in my feet when I had squashed them under my body for too long and the blood had run out. My mother said, something like that. I could tell that I had said the wrong thing, and that she found it exhausting trying to explain her illness to me. She spoke slowly, like she sometimes did on the days when she was too tired to get out of bed. I wished I could lay my head in her lap.

I slept a lot. My grandmother sent me to bed early and didn't often wake me up. She let me skive school and wrote absence notes for my teachers. She was very inventive. To me she said, what on earth are you going to learn there? With all the village idiots? Read a good book, you'll get more from that. She pressed her collection of the classics into my hands. But I preferred to read about people stranded on an island, or stories set in the future. I took the books and installed myself on the floor behind the armchair in the living room. My only friend was in the town. There was no one I wanted to see.

Once I gave my grandmother a picture I had painted. That's my dream house, I told her. Ten balconies, a slide from the bedroom to the swimming pool and four playrooms. But I didn't tell her about the most important thing. There was a switch with which I could electrify the house. Anyone who touched it from outside then would start to convulse. I imagined to myself how the children from the new school would try to knock at my window with their sausage fingers and how they would then be thrown back by the current. My grandmother was pleased with the picture. She said to me, perhaps I would be an architect one day. I should carry on drawing. Shortly after the evening news my grandmother would put her nightdress on and lock the front door. That was the sign for me to go to the bathroom. By the time I came out she would be lying in the big double bed and the covers on my side of the bed would be turned down a bit. Underneath the electric blanket was waiting, having been warming the mattress for half an hour. The mountain of bedclothes formed a soft, warm hollow around me. The cover radiated above me. I savoured the heat and quickly fell asleep.

My grandmother worked all day. She cooked, shopped, darned my clothes, and sometimes she had customers there whose hair she coloured or curled. She had taught herself, she said. Even the man from the garage came to her. He had frizzy hair like a black man, but he was blond. The frizzy hair came from my grandmother. Really, he said, my hair is as flat as a toad under a lorry. Sometimes I fetched newspapers from the garage for my grandmother. I liked the man from the garage. He always said things you had to laugh at.

The man from the garage talked a lot about my mother. I have known her longer than you have, little miss, he said. Do you want to know what she was like? She was a wild bumblebee with the face of an angel, even as a child. Still waters... I gave all the children sweets. But she always got a few extra. She was a sleep-walker, did you know that? She used to get up at night and walk around in the house. Your grandmother watched her go to the fridge and take out the milk and drink, with wide staring eyes. Your grandmother drew a line on the milk bottle and showed your mother the next morning that a finger of liquid had vanished. Your mother didn't remember having drunk it. Your grandmother got into the habit of locking the front door and slept peacefully once more. Your mother didn't seem to come to any harm when she wandered about at night. But then in June your grandmother woke up and saw that the locked front door was standing wide open. The key was on the inside, the child's bed was empty. She saw your mother in the garden from afar, her nightshirt was white. The boy next door was standing in front of her with his trousers down. Your grandmother now thought the sleep-walking was just a cover story. She chased the boy away, and gave your mother a clip round the ear. The lass swore she had woken up that very minute. Your grandmother didn't believe a word. Since then she always takes the key out of the lock at night. Later, when your mother was older, she used to climb out of the window. The lads on motorbikes would stop in the valley down below. The man from the garage stopped, he was waiting for a reaction from me, a nod, a *tsk*, an attentive 'yes?' But I was thinking about my grandmother's house keys. Every evening she locked the front door. While I was in the bathroom she hid the key.

My grandmother had lots and lots of cats, more than ten. They lived in a large cage made from wire mesh. They were lazy, fat cats, comfortable captivity was all they knew. My grandmother had built the cage in the shed. At night and in winter my grandmother brought the animals into the house. They had a room in the upstairs to themselves while we slept. Sometimes I crouched in front of the cage and watched the cats. They lay in the grass and sunned themselves. Butterflies landed right by their whiskers, the cats dozed impassively with eyes half-shut. I called their names. If a cat came over it was simply coincidence. They only came if they were hungry. Sometimes they miaowed. It sounded like a cross between children whining and sheep bleating.

My grandmother used to have just one cat. The flap in the front door, now shut, was a reminder of that. My grandmother hadn't kept the first cat inside. But unfortunately this cat lived for only half a year. Its successors also died on the main road down in the valley. After she had picked up cat number four from the side of the road as a bloody bundle, my grandmother didn't let the next cat out any more. She nailed the catflap in the front door shut.

Soon there were more than ten cats tearing around the house. My grandmother had taken in all the kittens who were otherwise going to be killed. The cats were only allowed to pace up and down on the balcony or in the top floor of the house. They sharpened their claws on the furniture.

To begin with the cats slept in bed with my grandmother. When I was visiting they would lie down around me. One night I accidentally squashed one cat's leg. It scratched my face. My grandmother was woken by my screams. She cleaned the wound and dabbed iodine on it. I looked like an Indian squaw. After this incident my grandmother built a cage. The cats were rehoused.

On the meadow in the valley, next to the fire station, there stood a giant red circus tent. My grandmother came with me to one of the performances. It was a small circus. They only had a llama and five goats. They made up for it with a tightrope walker though. She moved along the tightrope like it was a never-ending mossy woodland floor. She leapt, walked forwards, backwards, stretched one leg out to the side, she hopped without ever looking down. I was transfixed. I tried to copy her in the living room. I explained to my grandmother that I wanted to be an acrobat when I grew up. My grandmother laughed. When I announced I wanted to join the gymnastics club she wasn't laughing any more. Two girls from my class did gymnastics. I even knew already when the training was. I wanted to wear a shiny blue leotard too and dance on the beam, later I would switch to the tightrope. My grandmother was strictly against it. Certainly not, gymnastics was far too dangerous. I would get curvature of the back... I would never develop into a woman, the training was too hard. I didn't know what curvature of the back was, but it sounded like a dress cut low in the back, bare down to the bottom like the woman in the perfume advert. Never becoming a woman I also didn't think was so bad. But my grandmother wouldn't be swayed. Curvature of the back had nothing to do with dresses, it caused pain. And if I didn't become a woman I would never have any children either. I didn't think that was such a bad thing. She said, one day I would change my mind, then I would be grateful to her. I said my mother would have let me go. My grandmother shouted at me, my mother wasn't here. I slammed the door behind me angrily. It cracked the handle.

In the evening my grandmother would make me camomile tea. But I still played paratroopers at seven o'clock in the evening. I would jump off the fourth step and scream as I went. My landing made an almighty crash. I had to drink a second cup of tea. This time my grandmother added a clear liquid. Now the tea tasted bitter and I complained. She said a dash of the water did no harm, it just relaxes you. My eyelids grew heavy, I crept under the heated blanket. At night I apparently had wild dreams. I tossed and turned, tore the sheet from the mattress, threw the pillow onto the floor. In the morning, while still half asleep, I noticed my grandmother watching me. Normally she was already up and about in the house by the time I woke up. But today she was sitting on a chair by my bed. She lost no time. She said she would like me to stay with her, all the time. Did I not want to stay here too? After waking up I rarely put up any resistance. I nodded. My grandmother seemed relieved. She impressed on me that it wouldn't be a problem. We would go into the city, and there was a lady there, I just had to tell her that I wanted to stay here too. I thought of my mother, but I didn't ask if she would be there too. My grandmother gave me a kilt to put on and tied my hair back with a clasp. The woollen tights scratched. I couldn't pull them up properly, they hung between my legs. When I walked it felt like they would fall down any minute. We took the bus and then the train. My grandmother had put on a green hat and leather gloves. I spent the whole time looking out the window. I hadn't been in the city for a long time. Every tree that flashed past the train window amazed me. We didn't go to the flat where I had lived with my mother. My grandmother took me to a large building with a clock. We waited for ages in the corridor. I did slides on the floor. In full flow I skidded into my mother's feet. I got a shock. Her face seemed to have run. It looked like when I painted with watercolours and was too impatient to wait until the yellow was dry before I added the green. The shapes flowed into each other. Her eyes, her mouth, her nose had blurred. My mother took me in her arms. She said she had put on weight because of the tablets. Did I mind? I shook my head. She smelled different. Standing next to my mother was a lady with a briefcase. My grandmother came over to us and laid her hand on my shoulder. My mother said, Mama... it sounded like a plea. My grandmother nodded to her. It was for the best for all of us, she said to her, my mother needed calm. The lady with the briefcase said, you should weigh up all the options. At the present time... But my grandmother interrupted her and suggested they went in.

A man with long hair stayed behind to keep me company. We did a jigsaw in his office. The picture was nearly finished when a lady in a black gown came in. She said she was the judge. She asked why I was absent so often from school, whether my mother had made me hot lunches, what there was to eat at my grandmother's. I soon had enough of her questions, I said I was tired. She assured me it would soon be over. She left the room. When I opened the door I could see my mother and grandmother sitting at the back of the room. While we carried on with the jigsaw I listened to the voices next door.

The man with the long hair and I managed two puzzles and a game of Connect Four by the time the grown-ups were finished with their conversations. My mother and grandmother were standing together in the corridor. They hadn't seen me yet. As I walked up to them I could hear my mother speaking. She asked why my grandmother had told them she was not capable of looking after her child. Was she trying to take me away from her? She was my mother, no one would have me without her agreement. My mother went quiet when she saw me. She put on a smile. I was allowed to stay at Granny's for another six months, she informed me. Wasn't that nice? My grandmother added that Mama would come and visit me when she was feeling better. My mother looked at her. She was already feeling better, she insisted. The man with the long hair patted me on the head. I suspected they were hiding something from me. It must be to do with my mother's treatment.

At night I woke with a start. The darkness surrounding me was thick and sticky. I sat up in bed. I wondered what had woken me. My heart was beating loud. Suddenly I heard it. A penetrating scream, winding up like a siren. I didn't know if it was human or animal. The scream stopped sharply. Then after a while the scream started up again, then the voice wailed, almost like a baby. Silence. I listened spellbound. In the pauses between the screams I noticed my grandmother's regular breathing: she was asleep. Somewhere to my right in the darkness her nostrils flared. The screams came from outside, I could tell. They scared me. If whatever it was that was screaming like that had climbed into bed with me I would have died. Suddenly the screams turned into a cat hissing, and a second answered in the same way. The two cats seemed to be fighting. I heard them running. After they had disappeared there were no more screams. It took a long time for me to get back to sleep.

I thought about my mother: her short, bright fingernails. Before she changed the colour every week. I was allowed to paint her nails, but afterwards she would wipe it off again. I made a mess deliberately. I like the smell of the nail polish remover. When I was alone I would take the cotton pads out of the bin and sniff at them. Sometimes I even got my hands on the whole bottle. Then I would hide away in the bathroom. My grandmother had no nail varnish. I had almost forgotten what it was like living with my mother. Suddenly everything that had been bad didn't seem so terrible after all. The day when she had sold my bike because she needed the money was a long time ago. As were the days when she would lock herself in her bedroom and I could hear her crying through the door. She wouldn't let me in.

After the trip to court my grandmother sent me to school every day. She woke me up. I had to shower, rather than being allowed to doze in the bath till my fingers went wrinkly. The water pattered onto my belly, cold and unfriendly. I only held the shower head as high as my belly-button. I had goose pimples on my arms. In swimming lessons I wore small checked bikini bottoms with ties at the sides; I thought the matching top was unnecessary, but all the other girls wore swimming costumes. A few of them followed me round during break and whispered, didn't I have any money for a bikini top, and would I go swimming naked next time. I wasn't planning to. They weren't expecting me to answer. After a while the children left me in peace. Lessons were enough for me anyway. I had to continually be on my guard so that no one noticed how little I knew. I didn't understand what the teachers were talking about. They formed sentences with words that were familiar, but the meaning remained hidden. I soon worked out that my ignorance wouldn't be blown if I simply repeated their words back to them. Generally what teachers wanted to hear was something they had said three sentences ago. When I was called up I rattled off those words. The teachers were delighted. I got good marks. My grandmother didn't need to wake me up anymore – I got up of my own accord. She said she was proud of my success at school. But I should watch out. The next year at school wouldn't be a picnic and at some point my honeymoon period would be over. I tried not to think about autumn. I didn't want anything to change.

The man at the garage let me do gymnastics in his workshop. He put an old mattress on the floor to protect me. My hands sank into the mattress and I couldn't practice handstands on it, so I used the concrete floor and a wall for support. I could soon stand on my own. The man in the garage applauded. He took me with him to the druid stone. I told him the story of Abraham. How God put him to the test and commanded him to kill his only son. Abraham had been childless for a long time. He had prayed for this son for many years, and he doesn't want to lose him. Nonetheless he still lays the boy on the alter. Just as Abraham is poised to bring the knife down, the angel of the Lord halts him. The man from the garage said he had heard of it. Wasn't the story a bit too gruesome for someone of my age? I asked what my grandmother had been like as a child. The man from the garage had no idea. He thought about it for a minute and then answered that she was very lonely now. I had to look after her well. I didn't think that was necessary. She looked after me. The man from the garage said my grandmother only had me. And the cats. But they didn't answer to humans. I was a good girl, I brought my grandmother a lot of joy. I thought about the handstand. I knew that wouldn't have pleased my grandmother.

I tried to sew chain stitches while I walked. We had just had Textiles. As I came through the school gate I saw my mother on the other side of the street. She waved to me. I went over to her slowly. She took me in her arms. I looked around, in case anyone was watching us. But there were other mothers standing in front of the school and mine didn't stand out. She held me away slightly. We would soon be together again, she promised. She missed me. My mother took me to my grandmother's house. Then she had to go. My grandmother asked what was bugging me.

That night I decided to stay awake. After my grandmother had fallen asleep next to me in bed I got up. I opened the door to the cats. They weren't sleeping. With tails held high they prowled the room and miaowed at the window. They didn't seem to register me. They squeezed their bodies past each other, crowded onto the window sill and stared into the darkness. They were all females. There was nothing doing with them tonight. I went into the living room. A voice kept telling me I ought to go to sleep. My body needed sleep or I'd get ill. The more the phrase hammered in my brain the more I was proud to have overcome sleep. I wasn't tired. I wondered if I had ever been tired. I thought I could do without sleep entirely. I felt strong. I watched a film. But the people in it were speaking with two voices. They said something in German and like an echo another language sounded afterwards, a second person spoke in parallel with the first. That happened to my grandmother sometimes too, but she knew how to switch it off. There was a button on the remote control, I didn't know which one. I curled up in the armchair and pulled the woollen blanket around me. The noise of the television accompanied me into my dreams.

I woke up in a large, broad double bed, on the left, on the wall next to the mattress, hung the praying hands. I didn't know how I had ended up back in bed. My grandmother wasn't lying next to me, nor was she in the kitchen. The clock above the kitchen table said it was already midday. I slurped cornflakes soggy with milk from a carton. My grandmother came into the kitchen. She said, you'll get ill if you don't sleep. I noticed she had a scratch on her neck. She nodded happily when I asked for a sweet. The sun hung in the sky like a faded yellow crest in between grey clouds. The whole village was shrouded in haze. I didn't know what to do. I was afraid that everything would change again. It didn't matter if it was for the worse or not. So long as something stayed the same. I went to see the cats in the cage. The fat grey one let me stroke her. She purred like a very distant chainsaw. Soft and heavy she lay in my lap. But then the neighbour's dog came. He growled, the cat arched her back, dug her claws through my trousers into my thighs. I threw her down from my lap.

At the end of the six months my mother stood outside the front door. My grandmother was standing to one side behind the curtain and thought she was invisible. I opened the door before she could say anything. My mother came in, I was sent away. But I still heard my grandmother and my mother fighting. I ran on the spot, on the sloping lawn in front of the house. I did that to take my mind off it and because I knew that's how athletes build up strength. I could already do handstands, arabesques and dive rolls. I was just practicing the splits when the two of them appeared at the door. I scrambled to my feet. My mother took my hand. But I twisted out of her grasp and ran off.

Frosted Glass

Two rooms, kitchen, bathroom. The wallpaper still damp, the floor freshly glued, no furniture. On the seventh floor of a block of flats in Lichtenberger Straße. 'Small and cramped and well-intentioned,' thought Enna. 'The state supposedly had good intentions when they planned these flats. There isn't much left of the idea. Today the flats look soulless.' She nodded to the caretaker and murmured, 'Nice PVC, well fitted.' He pointed to the wall. 'Built-in cupboards, so big you could stick a child in them.' The sound of a welding machine came from next door. She suddenly had a desire for an old apartment with remnants of wallpaper on the walls, patches of mould, cracks which gaped, rattling windows where the neighbours could see in. Maybe she would have been better with that kind of place. She would have known where to start. But here? She could smear mud over the walls. She smiled. Did a flat come to life with dirt? She lifted her hand, put it on the window catch and contemplated her fingers, as if looking at them might tell her what she, Enna, would become here, in this flat. Resting on the window catch her hand looked like a poor exhibit in a museum, bloodless, inhuman. The judgement was too soul-destroying to accept. She turned away. Leaning on the window frame she took in the room. Behind her back her fingernails dug into the grey silicon between the glass and the frame. That had comforted her as a child, the soft malleability of plasticine. She walked along the corridor. On the right was the bathroom with

Turkish tiles, then the galley kitchen, behind that a tiny room, presumably the bedroom. Only the larger room lay to the east. All the doors had a pane of frosted glass in the middle. You could see the outline of objects behind it. The nurses' room in the hospital had a door like that. She could see the carer eating at the table from the corridor. She had enjoyed watching him. His squirrel posture, hunched forward, his arms tucked into his body, was familiar to her, although she hadn't been able to work out which of the carers it was. Noises came from the ward behind her. That's where her father's bed was. She had looked in on him.

  In the flat in Lichtenberger Straße there were neither objects nor people that she could discover behind the doors. She entered the living room. The caretaker in his blue dungarees stood in the door, blocking her way. It was her first viewing, there were certainly plenty more flats. But all the same she had the feeling that each rejection was a step backwards, giving up on the big plan. She opened the window. The cars on the four-lane highway sped by right in front of the house. The irregular flow of cars was regulated by the traffic lights at the corner. With the window open the living room was as loud as a launderette with ten machines on spin cycle. She stuck her head right out.

Alone in the bare flat, she lay awake at night. At times she imagined she was dreaming, but then she came to again immediately, tired and overwrought. She had rented the flat. It was central, there were green spaces, the rent was affordable. You could definitely come to like the rooms, she told herself. Then again: she could have moved into an area with older housing, the stage school was in the North. But she had been determined to find a flat immediately. She had signed for the first offer, she was flexible. She thought that suited her, 'a flexible young woman'. In a short sleep phase she dreamt about home, she recognised the pattern on the living room lamp. She had never dreamt about her father. He had been buried in March. She looked at the photo of him. She told herself the story of how he drove her over a seesaw in a wheelbarrow at the summer fete when she was four. She thought she remembered it stopping for a second before the plank tipped the other way and he wheeled her down. She had looked up at him from inside the wheelbarrow, he had pulled a scary face and threatened to tip her out. She had screeched with pleasure. She saw him in overalls on the building site for their house. She ought to have lots of memories, she had always lived at home. But when she tried to call up images they came only hesitantly. Later that night she dreamt of a man who resembled her father, but it wasn't him. He spoke differently. She woke up with the feeling that she had lost something in the dream. Without knowing what it had been. She tried to remember. She wasn't used to the flat yet. It only gradually dawned on her where she was. The stage school had given her a place, she had moved out, she had rented this flat. As her thoughts took order, it came to her like a flash of lightning, the memory of her father, of his death. The worst thing about it wasn't the loss. What was dreadful was all the things she had not done, thought, said. All at once there seemed to be a lot of them. She imagined that her father was sitting in the room next door, deep in one of his astronomy books. What would she say? More than usual? Probably not. She tried not to think about it. She got dressed.

After the rehearsal she bumped into an Arab man on rollerskates, pushing a tartan shopping trolley. Cardboard boxes peeped out, printed with pictures of battery-powered handheld vacuum cleaners. She reckoned he was in his early thirties. He came up to her shoulder, but the rollerskates made him taller. She was just standing in front of a shop, staring at the mannequins' feet and couldn't understand how she had got here. She always had problems after rehearsals. Sometimes she got on the wrong underground train or got to the counter and forgot what she wanted. She often regretted the fact that she didn't drive. The other students had told her that for an hour after performances actors were legally considered non compos mentis. They could murder, betray, steal. With no punishment, she imagined. Rehearsals were exempt from the rule mind you. The Arab asked her, 'Do you have the time?' She said, 'In theory... No.' He grinned, then pointed at her necklace with the silver locket on it. You could only make out the engraving of SOS from close up. She twisted the clasp of the locket and opened it. A tiny snake of paper fell out from the inside. 'These are the medical instructions in case I fall unconscious,' she explained to the Arab. 'Instructions? What for?' he asked. 'I'm diabetic.' That was a lie. She had forgotten to take the chain off after the rehearsal. The cry for help only applied until the stage exit, the diabetes was part of her role. *The Golden Child*, it was called, a contemporary play. The Arab asked, 'Do you know Georgia? The Black Sea? Shevardnadze? That's where my parents are from.' So he was Georgian. 'I sell table-top vacuum cleaners. Do you want one?' He ran one of the machines along her arm, without switching the suction on. She pushed him away, smiling. He asked 'Do you exercise? I also teach aerobics lessons.' She told him about her attempts at jogging along the canal. 'May I?' He grabbed her around the waist without warning, measuring with both hands. 'Stomach exercises would be good for you. Or are you pregnant?' She thought he was a bit impertinent, hesitated with her reply, then just shook her head. Today at rehearsal she had heard herself speaking again. From that moment on she hadn't been able to act. It had just been a read-through of the text. All the other students seemed to have noticed. But they were too considerate to say so. After the scene they avoided her. The Georgian would distract her. He was an experience, she could use that, maybe even to study a role. Every meeting, every experience was important. And where else would she get the experiences of a Georgian who sold vacuum cleaners on the street, who sailed over the asphalt on his rollerskates, probably fleeing the VAT men?

On the steps to the underpass he flicked the brake stopper on the roller skates down. It gave the impression of a clumsy ballerina *en pointe*. He clutched the handrail. On the station forecourt he motioned her over to a phone booth. 'Look,' he said. He had taken a handkerchief out of his trousers and wiped it over the receiver mouthpiece. He held the hanky in front of her nose. It was now discoloured and grey. 'You can catch all sorts, if you're not careful,' he informed her. 'All that dirt and the bacteria... You've never thought about that, have you?' She said, 'I've got a mobile.' They walked along the edge of the pavement. The street was lit up as bright as day, tourists, Africans with trays of goods for sale as well as large groups of youths streaming towards the station, or away from it. The Georgian asked her for her phone number. She wrote down ten digits. Her number had eleven.

She followed him into McDonald's at Zoo Station. On the first floor ten or twelve men were sitting together, most of them under forty. Enna assumed that they all came from the same state by the Black Sea. She was wrong. They did know the Georgian, but they spoke Russian to each other. Enna understood two or three words of greeting. The Georgian on his skates rolled from one to another, punching shoulders, shaking hands. The men eyed Enna indifferently, like they already knew everything about her. It annoyed her. She went off to fetch a milkshake. When she came back the Georgian rolled over to her and steered her to a table next to the group. He sat her down with her back to the group and sat himself down on the stool opposite. She felt she was being observed. He questioned her, where did she come from, how old was she, what did her parents do, did she still go to school. Sometimes she told the truth. She didn't say anything about the stage school. At one point he put his arm around her shoulder, but she turned away. She said she had to go to the toilet and stood up. She took her coat and bag. Without turning round she left the McDonald's. She hadn't felt like saying goodbye.

The head of the stage school stood at the window of her office and looked out. She asked Enna which dramatists she liked. Enna named two classic names, one representing political theatre, the other classical theatre, and for a third a new, unknown female playwright who wrote modern, topical, quick but dense plays, so people said. The head nodded her head slightly. Then she invited Enna. To hers on Sunday evening.

The head's apartment was in a neighbourhood with cobblestones and old street lamps lit by new bulbs. In the foyer of the house there was a circular opening which gave a view into the hallway of the house next door. The opening looked like an image in a mirror. On the other side, in the hallway of the house next door, the floor was also tiled black and white, the bannisters had the same brass knobs, the same intricate flower decorations. Enna stuck her hand through the hole to convince herself it wasn't a mirror. The front door on the other side opened. A dog ran past below the opening, barking. She quickly drew her hand back. She took the lift to the third floor.

Outside the head's door it smelled of onion soup. Her son opened the door and disappeared back into his room straight away. Enna could hear him playing guitar. The head called to Enna from the kitchen to come in, then came out herself. She went for air kisses. 'Is it cold outside?' She didn't expect an answer. Enna had brought a bottle of wine. The head put it to one side. It wouldn't go with the soup. There were no other guests. The two women ate alone in the living room. They sat at right angles to each other. The head ate without speaking.

By the time Enna got home it was nearly morning. Her feet throbbed. She had walked. Taking a taxi would have been too expensive. She closed the door behind her and put the chain on. Next to the phone were her photocopied scripts and her Aikido things for the class today. She called the office and spoke to the answering machine, saying she was ill and wouldn't come in today. She slept in. When she woke around three o'clock she had a dry mouth. Still lying down, she took a sip of water. She reached for the phone. It rang ten times before it was picked up. Enna said 'It's me'. Her mother sounded relieved. She said that the fire brigade had just been. One of the neighbours had set fire to a dried flower arrangement. The whole building still smelled of burning. It occurred to Enna that her mother often talked about strangers. Her mother only ever exchanged polite greetings with the neighbour when they passed each other. But she could still tell a lot of stories about her. As if the neighbour's life was important for her. Maybe it was too. 'You could have burned to death,' Enna said to her mother, who replied, astonished, 'What makes you think that?' She changed the subject. When she put the phone down her mother said, 'Take care of yourself.'

Enna rocked a bottle of schnapps in her arms. She was standing in front of a black backdrop. A young man next to her draped a hairdresser's cape around his shoulders and began to shadow box with open scissors. Enna spoke to the bottle. 'Do you know what's beautiful? It's not a place. It is an animal. Teeny-tiny, just a pupa. It creeps out of the ground at night, pushes the sand out of the way, climbs up a blade of grass and dries its long, transparent wings. Then it flies away. Do you hear that, it flies away. Shining little thing...' The young man suddenly jerked Enna's head back by her hair, forcing her to stare at him. 'Of all the whores, you're the dirtiest,' he yelled. 'Repeat after me: Of all the whores, you're the dirtiest.' She raised the schnapps above him and, with a scream, dashed the bottle on his head. The young man sank to the floor, although the bottle hadn't touched him. The drama students applauded. Enna and the young man climbed down from the stage.

'No-one in my family had anything to do with the theatre,' the head said. 'We have that in common. Of course, those were different times. Many things were harder back then, but things were also much clearer. Television, advertising, it didn't really exist then. Theatre was all there was.' Enna was just slipping into on a fox-fur jacket from the head's wardrobe. In front of the mirror she smoothed her hair back from her face. She liked the jacket. She threw it on the bed. She held up some corduroy trousers. The head wasn't paying any attention to her. 'I had a child because I thought it would be nice to be able to live without always thinking 'me, me, me.' He is eighteen now. When he was two I realised that I was saying 'you' but I meant 'me'. I tried to change. I don't actually believe in change,' the head said and dismissed everything she had said with a wave of her hand. Enna saw it. She gazed through the mirror at the head for a long time. She saw the red marks on her neck. Enna asked 'Are you sure you don't need all these any more?' The head nodded. Enna stroked the material on the cord trousers. The head said, 'It will definitely suit you.' Enna said, 'The material reminds me of a jacket my father had.' The head asked, 'What was he like, your father?' Enna didn't answer. The zip on the trousers was stuck. She tugged impatiently at the catch. The head was waiting for Enna to say something else. But Enna silently put the shirts and blouses back in the wardrobe. She left the trousers lying.

The new teacher, a director from Bielefeld, didn't introduce himself. The students were familiar with his name. 'I am going to stage a world premiere with you,' he announced. 'A fragmentary drama by a young Spaniard. There are no set roles, only scraps of sentences. We have to search for the characters. If it goes wrong we won't find individuals, just clichés. But if it does work, you won't just have interpreted the play, you will have created it!' Enna had heard about the artistic debacle which was the reason the director had had to flee to them. He didn't look exhausted. He looked like someone you wanted to please, because he beamed back at you. They had all read the piece. The director handed out new versions. He had tried to bring out particular voices, he said. But he was open to suggestions. Four students voiced their ideas the day after. Enna said nothing. They began rehearsing. The weighting of the gradually crystallising roles arose, according to the director, 'from the personal dynamic in rehearsal.' Enna secretly translated to herself: whoever shouts loudest gets to stand at the front. The woman that Enna was supposed to portray mostly loitered at the edge of the stage, talking about her hair all the time, and the job she had lost, moreover she coveted another woman's husband. After two weeks of rehearsals Enna's text had been cut in half. The director said, 'You possess a great physicality, you must use it!'

During the lunch break Enna and the head met at the canal. They walked upstream. 'I don't know what he wants. I don't know where to start with my role,' said Enna. 'How can he not see that? This woman's every movement convulses me. I can quite understand why Agathe wants to kill her.' Agathe had become the main role. 'My figure doesn't speak to me!' The head replied, 'A good actor makes something of every role.' 'But I don't have one any more. I dance. That's all.' The head looked at her thoughtfully. 'The director thinks very highly of you. I will have a word with him.'

The premiere took place on a Friday evening. The theatre was sold out. The debacle had made the director famous. The audience had come because of him. They wanted to know if he would go under once and for all. Enna was now playing the second main role. She had a lot of text. Once she threatened to freeze, but her partner helped her and she skipped the lines.

The public applauded longest for the girl who had taken over Enna's previous role. Enna counted the seconds. It was three times as long as she had got. At the aftershow party she sat down in a corner with the fox-fur jacket and a bottle of water. The head appeared in front of her. 'Are you pleased?' Enna said, 'Yes, of course. I'm just a bit overwhelmed by everything, that's all.' The head replied, 'It's a drama school, isn't it? You can stop acting now, the play is over.' She laughed encouragingly. Enna looked away.

The escalator led steeply into the depths, it seemed to go on for ever. Initially Enna had hesitated before taking the first step onto the stairs. In the past few weeks she now strode quickly onto the escalator, jostled forward like on any other underground system. This time she stood still. On the escalator opposite, going up, she saw the Georgian. He was looking straight ahead, his collar turned up, his shoulders hunched up to his ears. He was freezing. He felt her gaze on his back and turned around. He seemed not to be wearing rollerskates. She turned away.

She had had a fight with the head. Everyone had witnessed it at the aftershow party. She was going to leave her the fox-fur jacket there, out of anger, but it was too cold for that. She would hand it back tomorrow. Best to do it at one o'clock, when the head would be teaching. Her son would be there to take the jacket in. 'Childish, ungrateful and full of herself,' the head had called her. Before that Enna had snapped, 'Stop sticking your nose in my affairs!' It was the allocation of roles which sparked it. 'You wanted a different role!' 'But you and the director, you should both have known better! Neither I nor the girl I swapped with had enough time to learn the new lines.' The head had given her an enquiring look. 'Are you serious?' When Enna said yes, the head lost her temper, called her every name under the sun, and a bad actor and colleague to boot. Enna had answered, 'You should know what you're talking about. After all, you're doing what any good actress does when they're inundated with offers... All the great talents would teach if directors would let them, wouldn't they?' The head suggested she stay at home for two weeks. After that they would see.

She stood on the platform and waited for the underground. The station was almost empty. The display flashed and she could hear the train approaching in the tunnel. The headlights were already visible. Suddenly someone shoved her from behind, she fell on the tracks. The train hurtled towards her, the noise was deafeningly loud. She lay there like she was paralysed. The train drove right over her. She felt her bones shatter, her blood spurted against the station attendant's cabin.

Every time she was waiting on a platform she saw this scene before her, just like she did this time. The image forced itself upon her, she couldn't suppress it. But now she watched the daydream as if it were someone else's fears, from outside. She had got used to it. The thought of her own annihilation no longer scared her. She stepped closer to the edge of the platform every time, she thought that was a good sign. She threw an old receipt that she found in her trousers into one of the rubbish bins on the platform.

She couldn't get to sleep that night. She made a bet with herself about which of the windows lit up opposite would go out first. She only won when there were two left. The last window was on the first floor, and the light came from a television. The tenant had probably fallen asleep in front of the box. Her mobile showed five in the morning. Her father was sitting at the kitchen table. He had the newspaper lying in front of him. His face was just an outline. But she knew he wasn't smiling. She had just told him he could keep the book. He should open his mouth if he wanted to say sorry, and not let others speak for him, dead poets. He had bought her André Gide, *The Counterfeiters*, and laid the book on her bed without comment. She had found it there. She understood. That was meant to make up for their stupid fight that afternoon. She didn't even know what they had been fighting about any more. She didn't want to make up though, not like that. There was toast on the table in front of her father. The jam on top wobbled like it was alive. She knew she was in the wrong, that she should accept his offering, but she still couldn't forget her anger. She wanted to seize him by the shoulders and shake him. Instead she was suddenly swimming in red jelly, sticky, impenetrable. The sugary substance entered her mouth, her eyes, her ears. She struggled to stay on top. All of a sudden her resistance disappeared. She fell into a hole with no bottom.

A few hours later she woke up properly. She began to pack her removal crates. She found the book, *The Counterfeiters*. She put it next to her mattress. She hadn't read it yet. She had a sudden urge to go running. She ran the length of the canal, until the world began to pulse, and then back. Still out of breath she made a resolution. She would stop the acting, start something new, dancing perhaps. She felt better. She got takeaway fish and chips from the Irish pub on the corner. She sprayed vinegar over the greasy potato pieces. She would have preferred to eat only the beer batter off the fish. She wrote to the head. She said she was sorry. She gave the letter and the fox-fur jacket to the head's son. He took a while to realise who she was, this strange woman at the front door.

A poster of Herman Hesse hung on the wall. The sketched Hesse head was swallowing a flame, or spitting it out. Enna couldn't make it out exactly. She lay naked on the narrow bed under the poster. She had chucked the fox-fur jacket down next to her. The head's son pressed his head into her inner thighs. 'Why is the hair there so much thicker and more coarse?' he asked, and felt his tongue with his finger. Enna pulled him to her. They kissed. He had a small goatee. 'I like your dark skin,' he said then. 'And you have a clear face. When you have no make-up on, it's hardly visible. That's how clear it is. It's all perfectly obvious. It couldn't be any different.' Enna went to the desk and sat down next to the computer keyboard. She said, 'I would never have noticed you on the street.' The lad came over to her. He had a large scar on his belly. He didn't like it when she touched him there. Enna stroked his shoulders and arms. 'I have the feeling I can't do anything wrong with you,' she said.

Her father's name was written on a cast-iron plaque. There were hundreds of identical plaques next to his. All the cremation urns stood in a row on the long wall which bordered the cemetery. Enna had brought flowers. She laid them on the ground in front of the wall. Then she stared at the plaque. The head's son came closer and asked, 'Do you want to be alone?' She said, 'I don't mind you being here.' He added, 'It's perhaps not the best place for remembrance.' Behind the cemetery wall was a tennis court. They could clearly hear the plopping sound of the balls. On the tram Enna rested her head on the lad's collar.

'I miss you,' Enna said. 'I miss you more than I can say. When I open my eyes the first thing I know is that you are not here. And everything that was, is being taken from me. It turns in circles like a branch on the river, just before the waterfall. I recorded your voice. But the more I hear it, the more unfamiliar it becomes to me. I gaze at your photo, but you are slipping away from me. I talk to those who knew you, but that is not the same. I wish you were here.' She paused. The curtains in the room were closed. The drama students were squatting on the floor. The head said, 'What inner pose are you striking? Show us.' Enna cowered on the floor, hugged her knees and raised her head to the ceiling. She saw two of her fellow students whispering. As she was going out, the head asked Enna to come to her office. Her expression was neutral. The head went on ahead. Her shoes squeaked as she walked. Enna packed her things.

Enlightenment

We are waiting for the last blind. Three of the high windows are already blacked out. Slowly, humming, the fourth blind descends. I rummage for my exercise book in the dark. The classroom for the biology lesson is in tiers, one row of desks per step. The lowest point is the teacher's desk. We are sat on high at white lab benches with built-in sinks. The first thing we did was turn on the taps. We were dissecting cows' eyes at the time. We washed the retina in the sinks. The benches in the biology room are bolted down, the stools aren't. Fabian next to me was tipping back on his. The teacher is standing behind us by the slide projector, she is setting it up. In the front row Michael presses Julie's hand onto the top of his thigh, she digs her fingernails into his jeans, painfully, he looks straight ahead at the projector's light spot. He can feel Julie's nails, but it is her, not him, who emits a squeak. Very quietly, so that only he can hear it. We sense the sound, it is quiet like bats peeping. The pitch is too high for the teacher's ear, she can't hear it. 'All hatches battened down,' Benno announces from the main switch for the blinds. The teacher, Frau Wolters, nods absent-mindedly, she is lost in the world of her slides, which she is carefully slotting into the projector in order. Rumour has it that the teacher is divorced, her son ill, heart problems. Before Christmas Frau Wolters lets us write book lists, she buys presents for her nephews and nieces based on what we put down. She thinks we know our stuff. During lessons the teacher puts on slide shows, they are her favourite.

'Red and yellow asters...dominant, recessive...filial generation.' Before the show we revise Mendel's Laws. I've had the facts of life three times, officially. The first time in primary school, then again age twelve in our last year, one more time in high school, and now follows the advanced course, genetics. The final examination is the gynaecologist. The class is going to go, in private. The teacher thinks this is a good idea. But beforehand she shows us hermaphrodites and other genetic defectives. The slides are already quite tatty. The first image appears on the screen over the board. It shows a young woman. 'That is Anna Ramirez from Mexico City at the age of eighteen,' the teacher says. 'A completely normal, pretty young woman.' We see a delicate girl with a black ponytail, probably photographed in the seventies. She is wearing a white skirt and has a winning smile. The researcher who took the photo must have been nice to her. Or maybe it was her then boyfriend who stood behind the lens and called encouragingly. 'Hey baby, smile! Just for me! Say: shesellsseashells!' Anna Ramirez is happy, young, a girl you could take for a drive in a convertible, one who belongs everywhere.

Michael and Julie fight silently in the dark. They yank at each other viciously, although everyone knows that nothing ever happens between them. They need the classroom as an arena, on their own it's more difficult. We are aged fourteen going on fifteen. The boys have their first shaving cuts on their faces, the girls have them on their legs. We breathe the white dust which dances in the light of the projector. Tacos and tequila, that's all I associate with Mexico. I yawn with my mouth wide open. The teacher pauses too long on this image. She stands there as if Anna Ramirez is telling her personally about her Mexican homeland, sun, sea, caramba. Frau Wolters swallows. She presses the button on the remote control. It clicks, and the next picture slides into the ray of light. On the second slide Anna Ramirez is twenty five years old, married. Her husband has his arm around her. Benno makes gagging noises. Presumably that means that he doesn't like the look of the husband. I stare at the screen. Anna Ramirez has seemingly got a bit fatter. It's a full-length portrait again. She looks heavier in the picture, but not softer. Her nose looks like it has been broken several times. Otherwise I don't see anything of note. The hermaphrodites were more interesting than Anna Ramirez.

There are two empty stools between me and my neighbour at the bench, Fabian. He is right-handed, I write with my left. My elbows would get in his way if we sat too close. So that is our unspoken agreement. The idea of swapping sides doesn't occur to us. Then there wouldn't be a problem. Valeska in the front row whispers to Silke. After school they often go into town together. They apparently get up to all sorts of mad things. They slip into big hotels, use the pool and sauna without paying. They order expensive cocktails at the bar and give a false room number. One time they showed me a hand towel they had nicked. That was after I had written their picture description for art class.

The teacher clicks the remote control again. The switch in her hand looks like a self-timer for a camera. The next slide moves into the ray of light. Anna Ramirez is thirty years old in it, she has been 'discovered'. It is a clinical portrait, lit like a criminal's in front of a white prison wall. The researchers call Anna Ramirez's illness 'creeping masculinisation of the physique,' her bones suddenly start growing again, a defective gene is to blame. The giant bones make her figure more bulky. Her face grows broader, her nose more stumpy, her features blur, she is no longer recognisable. She wouldn't just have problems at a school reunion. She has turned into someone else, something else, indefinable, because of her appearance. 'The change only affects her appearance,' the teacher says. 'The only thing that grows is the cartilage. The organs remain unaffected.' It puts me in mind of a magazine report in which women disfigured in accidents were portrayed. Before, after. They had all been left by their partners, however much they tried to live up to the old picture. With wigs, make-up, operations.

On Thursday we go to the gynaecologist. Alina has called in sick, a day beforehand just to be on the safe side. She knows Doctor Scheer. I was standing next to her in the phone booth in the school yard when she made the appointment. Her period hadn't come, she had to do something. The first years kept flinging the door wide open, I kept them out. Alina's voice sounded very small, she almost toppled over when she repeated the time again, 'Tomorrow, ten o'clock?' Our geography test was scheduled then. She didn't do the test. The teacher shook his head as he entered her absence in the register. It was touch and go whether she would fail this year.

The gynaecologist's practice is housed in one of the blocks on Büchnerplatz. The entrance to an underground garage gapes in the middle of the asphalt. There are no benches, no plants or trees on the square, just concrete and stone. The last decent shop closed a year ago, now instead of expensive clothes the building sells bronze figures and plastic liners for ornamental ponds. During recent months cheap chains of shops have moved in around the square, I can read the signs from the window, 'Benny's Bargains', 'Penny Paradise', 'Discount Brands'. The gynaecologist has also only recently moved here. He greets each of us with a handshake, firm and confident. He sizes us up over the top of his semi-circular glasses. He probably detoxes on holiday. Detoxing and cycling fast with a helmet on, that would suit him. He looks solid, fit. I imagine him jogging with his white coat on in the birch grove behind our house, taking long, springy steps, drawn out in slow motion and flying a banner behind him, '*Mens sana...!*' The receptionist is young. As we occupy the entrance in the surgery, she quickly picks up a plastic tube full of urine from the counter and disappears into the laboratory. The doctor directs us into the waiting room, Frau Wolters and he want to discuss the format in private outside. A woman with grey curls is still waiting for her appointment, the doctor reassures her. She nods amenably and immerses herself in 'Tina' magazine. We make her uncomfortable. Benno reads out loud from one of the women's magazines. 'What is timeless? Femininity!' He laughs. No-one knows what he is laughing at. Michael joins in. Valeska whacks him on the back of the head with her hand. The old woman takes her glasses off and polishes them on the hem of her cardigan.

Doctor Scheer calls us into the treatment room. No-one wants to stand in front. The chair looks like a witch-hunter's instrument. There is a photo of a landscape on the wall. A forest stream in summer, the sunlight falls in rays through the leaves on the trees. The photograph hangs right next to the chair. The patients can see it if they turn their head away from the doctor. Alina probably looked at it, I think. The thought makes me feel unwell. In the corner is a screen, its panels are printed with Japanese temples. Alina must have got changed behind the partition as well. The only place to put her jeans, tights, underwear would have been on the stool next to it. She must have appeared in front of the doctor 'bottomless'. Consultation precedes the examination, sometimes the patients sit down again afterwards in the armchair in front of the desk. A grey paper towel, like the ones for drying your hands in public toilets, lies on the seat. The leather is not to get grubby underneath the naked women. I look at the family photos next to the pencil sharpener on the desk top. I wonder whether the doctor examines his own wife. Behind the screen are two more boxes of paper tissues. Perhaps Alina wiped herself after the procedure with a tissue, took a sanitary towel from the box. I wonder how she felt after the curettage. Relieved? Sad? We have never spoken about it. I don't want to ask her, she has been very standoffish recently.

The treatment chair faces the window, they must have a good view from the block of flats opposite. There are blinds, but at the moment they are pulled up. The doctor is still explaining how an examination is conducted and demonstrating the instruments. The speculum to look at the cervix, long spatulas for the smears. He also shows us the forceps. Jokingly, he remarks that some of us had probably felt those, to judge by our lopsided faces.

After the visit the young receptionist serves us cans of Coke and lemonade. I can taste the aluminium in the fizzy liquid. We have taken up position between the hydroponic plants in the entrance area of the surgery. Some of us are standing, others squat on the floor, a few are rocking on the cantilevered chairs. A heavily veiled woman pushes past behind us with her husband. It is a community practice. The gynaecologists are carrying on with their work while we are looking round. 'Having a woman in the team is particularly good for such cases,' Doctor Scheer explains, pointing a finger in the direction of the veiled woman. 'I wouldn't be allowed to examine Muslim women, even blindfold.' Frau Wolters thanks him on our behalf for the invitation. Doctor Scheer acknowledges her remarks with a nod. His speech is short. 'There is nothing to be frightened of. It's all a question of mindset, tensing up leads to pain, in my profession psychology is a good half of it. I applaud Frau Wolter's idea to bring a whole class here. Even for the gentlemen among you it is certainly interesting to see what happens in women's clinics. You may ask questions now. Please don't be shy.' Frau Wolters has to start us off. She had anticipated our silence and in our last class she collected anonymous questions on pieces of paper. She unfolds the first note. I spy large, round handwriting like Bärbel's, who wears Gucci. 'Do you get fat if you take the pill?' The answer comes back like a shot. 'No, absolutely not. That's complete nonsense... thought up by someone who doesn't know what they are talking about. If one in a hundred girls puts on a few pounds, then it's more likely to be because she is allowed to stay out longer at night on the pill and therefore eats more pizza.' Frau Wolters reads out the next note. 'How high is the risk of getting infected by AIDS?' Doctor Scheer smiles. 'I'll happily look up the figures and pass them on to your teacher. But from my own experience in practice I think I can say that AIDS represents only a minor threat to you. Compared with pregnancy and other sexually-transmitted diseases. Let's put it this way: you don't know any black Africans, do you?'

I sit there and have a thousand questions, but none of them want to come out. I would like to ask what makes you love someone, why and for how long. I know the evolutionary answer already, I want another one. What signs mark when love is born and when it dies, that would interest me, and how you can put love to rest. I crumble one of the clay balls from the hydroponic troughs. When the questions run out, the doctor disappears back into his lab. He comes back with a kind of specimen jar. He passes it round. There is a tiny child swimming in formaldehyde. Now Doctor Scheer speaks more slowly than before. 'Abortion should be the last option. It is not a good option. Come to me before then. There are lots of ways to prevent that.' A few pupils pull faces in disgust. The foetus has webbed fingers. It looks like a tiny, wise old man, so bent and wrinkled. It looks like it is thinking.

We take the number 18 bus back to school. It's the end of the shift in the works, the workers crowd the bus. We stand. In the crush Michael dares to grab Julie's hand. He squeezes it way too hard. When he has to let go going round a corner I can see the white imprints of his fingers on the back of her hand. Benno and the others are bellowing this year's summer hit, Eternal Flame. They can't hit the emotional highs. I look out the window. The bus is stopping at the shopping centre when I spot Alina. She is wearing her red anorak, I can recognise her by it even from a distance. She ought to stay at home if she's skiving, the teachers often go to the shopping centre, it's right next to the school. Alina walks past the pub where we often meet. The shops are shut during the day. She is just going to turn the corner but her sleeve gets caught on one of the bars on the window, it pulls her back involuntarily. It looks comical. I can't help laughing, even though I don't want to. Alina doesn't see me, she frees her jacket from the bars, her movements are jumpy, it takes a while. The bus doors shut. Alina disappears behind the back of the pub. The teacher comes up to me. 'What's actually wrong with Alina?' she asks. She was standing with her back to the window. She can't have seen Alina. 'Flu?' I suggest. 'Like everyone...' The teacher looks in the direction of the shopping centre. 'Yes, it's that time again, don't you think?' 'It's the bad weather,' says Frau Wolters. 'Nothing really helps. Pass on my greetings to her and tell her to get well soon. She's been ill so often recently. I hope she'll be better soon.' She falls silent, and because she realises she has said too much to just walk away like that, she adds, 'Next lesson we'll be starting neurobiology. It's a compulsory exam subject. It wouldn't be a bad idea if you all start reading around already.' I don't believe it.

The bus stops with a judder in front of the school. We get out. Inspectors check the tickets at the door. We have a group ticket. We go unchallenged to the grammar school. In the school yard stands the modern Kant monument. The spikes of concrete arranged in a circle point outwards, they look like the Statue of Liberty's crown. With a lot of imagination the monument could be a site for occult rituals, a modern Stonehenge with pillars of cement instead of menhirs. No-one has dared to graffiti the monument yet. The bell goes for breaktime. Pupils and teachers push open the doors one after the other and blink in the sunshine. I stand at the foot of the steps. I don't feel like going up.

Other People's Windows

Last summer a man said to a woman, I love you. The two of them were sitting in a café in a small German town. The town is so small it doesn't even have a name of its own. It shares it with another place. The woman stared at the sun, the man said it again, I love you. He wondered if he had struck the right tone. His lips were rough, he ran his tongue over them. A swallow swooped over the asphalt in front of the town hall. The woman didn't speak. She rubbed the sleep from the corner of her eyes with her forefinger, her face lengthened as she did so, her closed mouth formed a silent 'Oh!' The woman had only just got out of bed, and had staggered to the café with the man, she hadn't reckoned on such an opening shot. At heart everything was very simple, they were floating on a steady stream. They would be each other's assurance, trust each other, entwine like the ivy which envelops a house. That's how their love would grow, dense and green, until no light could penetrate. One or both of them would reach for the secateurs, and in the end all that would be left would be a pile of branches on the ground. The woman thought all of this, but she didn't know what to say. She would have liked to murmur something, something soft, tender. But the birch pollen which had spun into her coffee seized her voice and so she coughed. She found it difficult enough holding together one person. How would she manage when there were two of them? The man must have been afraid too, probably afraid of the emptiness in the morning. To chase it away he said I love you too soon. Did he even know what he was saying? Did she? The woman scratched the back of her hand and hummed a song, for reassurance. It was 'Daisy, Daisy, give me your answer do,' if I am not mistaken. The woman would have happily sat in silence for ever. She wanted to linger in this moment. She knew the man was waiting for an answer. The man recited to himself the words he hoped to hear her say. She read the words on his forehead, but she didn't say them out loud. Instead she said: I had a dream. But she hadn't actually dreamt at all. I dreamed that the house was moving, it was running. I was on the top floor and I was scared that the building was going to fall in. The man thought 'fall down', the phrase was 'fall down', not 'fall in', wasn't it? He wasn't sure, but he hoped that 'fall in' was an omen in his favour. He said, your bladder was probably to blame. You needed to go to the toilet in your sleep and couldn't, the suppression re-emerged in your dream, that's how Freud explains it. He cursed himself, for with this remark the conversation had taken a wrong turn. And yet he had just said something, more than that: he had laid himself open. He felt exposed. He spread butter on his roll a second time, the jam in the little bowl in front of him was already drying out. The woman called, can we have the bill please! She was astounded: the waiter heard her the first time. The man at the table in the café looked at her. The woman remembered that he looked attractive when he was sad. He looked attractive now, too. His eyes were light and clear, his eyebrows undefined like a small child's, they always seemed to be raised. The woman rummaged for her purse. A tiny black beetle scurried across her bag. She flicked it off with her fingernail. While the woman settled the bill, the man solved his dilemma. In his mind he supplied the answer that she had failed to give him. The result didn't discourage him.

The man set off for the station. After he had left the table in the café the woman thought about the night before. She thought, papardelle with anchovies. She thought, little fish. She wanted to think that everything was right. The words, the gestures, they meshed like the teeth of a zip. Rrrrip, open and shut, like a fan. You-me, me-you, memeyouyou, youmemeyou. They were sitting on a fallen log in the woods. A light-blue sign glowed in the dusk. 'Trim trail,' he read out to her. Underneath a stick man in black was running towards the edge of the sign. The man and woman giggled at the sound of their stomachs, which seemed to be answering each other. They slapped at midges. One was sitting on his elbow, it stuck its proboscis into his skin. The man and woman watched as the midge sucked. He claimed that you didn't end up with itchy lumps if you didn't disturb the insect. They only injected poison when they were interrupted before they had finished their meal. The midge drank its fill of his blood. Finally it was done and flew away. The woman felt the cold evening air on her back. Soon afterwards his midge bite began to itch. He forced himself not to scratch.

The woman lived twenty kilometres from the small town. They had only come there for breakfast and because of the train station. The man wrote her a card at the ticket office. He had posted it even before he departed.

Dearest,

I recently read under a picture showing a young person's eye, 'Are you worried about getting older? A TB patient in the Third World would be pleased about it.'

There is only one eye pictured on the poster. The woman appears to have only one eye, the writing is similarly unbalanced – the picture is cropped, the text upsets our perspective. The small print reveals what can help. It contains a bank sort code.

I read this, thought about it for a bit, and yet I knew: if I can be good for someone, then it's for you and not for unknown lungs.

> Forgive me, I'm sermonising. Yesterday you touched me and today I am alone. That's hard to comprehend. I'm not even trying. M.

The woman took the card from her letter box the next morning. She was a teacher and on her way to school. She pulled out a red pen and scribbled between and next to the lines the man had written:

> Love is the loneliest business in the world. All the customers pay in foreign currency to a voiceless computer with big eyes. It isn't sad. Just odd. F.

The card was now nearly completely covered with the two competing sets of handwriting. The woman's capricious hand, which sometimes leant to the right, sometimes to the left and missed out letters, impatiently skipped syllables, filled all the blank space the man had left. His regular, old-fashioned and elaborate script was encircled by her hasty letters. Thus completed and pacified, the woman put the card in the school photocopier. Although she professed to send the card back immediately, she secretly wanted to hold onto what the man wrote to her after all. She copied both sides. The photo faded a bit. The card showed the unadorned side of the Rhine, where the Lorelei on her rock had swept sailors to their death. The woman sent the card back to the man's home address, six hundred kilometres away from where she lived.

But the card didn't catch the man at home, he was on the road again, washed up in Wiesbaden. He had interrupted his business trip here and was waiting for a connection in order to travel back to the woman. He didn't care if he blew his job for it. He was working on a new brochure for the Youth Hostel Association. He was supposed to be writing about the oldest of their hostels, which was in Altena. But rather than going to the Rhineland, an Intercity would take him to the woman in two hours. He passed the time until then in the theatre café. He watched old women in thick fur coats picking up their opera tickets for the evening, excitedly waving their manicured gnarled fingers around and getting tangled up in dogs' leads. The man counted four beaver furs and two minks. Using his mobile phone he called his next door neighbour. She was a student who had a soft spot for him. She kept an eye on his letterbox while he was away. Today she had fished out the postcard sent back by the woman. The man asked her to read out what it said. She began with his words, he hastily interrupted her. Obediently the student restricted herself to the woman's annotations. The man listened attentively. All that remained in his memory were the missing 'dear' and 'All the customers pay in foreign currency'. The rest of what she had written merged in his mind into a vague missive whose emotional colouration he placed somewhere between violet and duckbill yellow. Those colours were too uncertain for him to go to them, he decided. A miniature poodle's yapping jolted him out of his thoughts. The animal was standing right next to him. The man reached for the biro again and noted down on the café napkin:

> My love, would you suspect what was happening if they hacked off your arms and legs?. What would remain of you? What would remain of us? This is suggestion and question in one. Stage it on your personal menu, as usual.
>
> I am going to go to the river Lenne. Do you know why? I wrote that you hardly answer, everything else remains unsaid. Is that to go on forever?
>
> I just discovered that we are living in a time of 'subtle suspicion'. Apparently irony is the sweet poison of our language, it makes words disintegrate into uncertainty. That's the divination of a ruddy-cheeked farmer's kid from West Virginia in the weekly news. I have reason to believe him. Would that thou could say the same of me. I wish, M.

It's almost a decade since the man could have been called youthful. In the youth hostel in Altena he had to sign in as a 'senior'. He spent the night in one of the communal rooms, as a geography teacher and her girlfriend were already dozing in the group leaders' room. They were in charge of a noisy eighth-grade class, whose nocturnal pillow fights annoyed the man in the dormitory. While he lay awake he thought of the woman. He had no idea what subjects she taught. He hoped he would be able to ask her soon. The man slept badly in the top bunk under the brown beams on the ceiling. The next morning he bumped his head on the sloping ceiling above his mattress. At the breakfast buffet, a white table with a Formica top, he accidentally poured peppermint tea on his wholemeal bread. The man's head hurt. He was tired, aggravated about his wet bread and hungry, because the school group had already snaffled all the rolls and were playing catch with them. The man stared at their spotty faces, listened to them shouting. They were showing off, every throw became a chat-up line. The man sighed and thought about the brochure he was supposed to put together. Altena in the Rhineland was an industrial town, grey in winter and also in the summer. The chimneys funnelled the steam from the smelting metal up into the clouds that surrounded the castle hill. The tiny youth hostel was in the inner courtyard of the fortifications. The timber-framed house was where the servants had slept in olden times.

The man had visited the town once before, twenty four years ago. As a member of the young ramblers. It had been his first trip. In the winter of 1979 he was eleven years old. Back then there was precisely two shower cubicles in Altena. They were outside the actual youth hostel. Shivering with cold he had run down the icy steps outside the house, dashed into the cubicle, and hoped that there was still warm water left. To save water and time they had showered in pairs. He had stood in the ice-cold cabin with a boy whose name he had forgotten. They had splashed each other with cold water. Suddenly the other boy had turned the tap off. He had thought they were finished showering and fished for his handtowel. But the other boy had begun to soap himself. The man was still shocked to think about it. For eleven years he had believed it was enough to blast water onto his body. No-one had ever told him that the dirt on it was more stubborn than that. He had been ashamed. He snatched the soap from the other boy like his life depended on it. The other boy asked him if he had lice. The man hoped that the woman would only hear his version of the episode. With pride and humour he would tell the story of his ignorance then. He also thought up a romantic love scene which he located in Altena behind the shower cubicle's door made of planks of wood. With this invented childhood memory he would put the picture right.

Meanwhile the woman was kicking a pile of leaves next to a kiosk at the Schlachtensee lake; she sent the leaves spiralling up into the air. It was the beginning of November, the sun was shining over a red gold and green weekend idyll. It was unnaturally warm for this time of year. The trees were reluctant to shed their leaves. There were even a few bees swarming around. The temperatures forced them to. But they didn't find any blossom, so instead they flocked to any patch of colour that came near. The woman was wearing red. She forced herself not to flap her arms at the bees. She knew that would be silly. She didn't want to be silly. She was meeting another man.

Anxiously she walked up and down in front of the discounted flowers next to the zebra crossing on the lakeside road. The man was too late. That wasn't what was making the woman anxious though. She told herself she had no grounds for concern. Why should a meeting with another man automatically lead to betrayal. Whom could she betray in any case? The man? Herself? The meeting? If it had been a class test, she would have answered the question following a simple logical framework. In her head she preferred to pull viewpoints to and fro, like heavy velvet curtains, open and shut. The scenarios that unfolded became more and more confusing. There were too many unknowns. The woman's problem was that she always thought everything through to the end. If she looked at a Sachertorte, she would see weight gain, heart attack and premature death. When she saw a pretty, cheap dress it screamed at her: child labour. There was no cure for her. She remembered medicines by their side effects.

Finally the date appeared. The man's panting seemed forced to the woman. His Ford had apparently broken down on the city motorway. Getting it moving again had taken a long time. The woman showed understanding, but presumed that the Ford had in reality been a warm, soft body in the man's bed which had insisted that he, rather than the car, stayed put. She cursed herself for waiting. In the half hour she had been kicking her feet against the island of flowers for nothing she could have taken the washing out of the machine, for example. Instead she would pull crumpled and clammy blouses from the drum this evening. She would stand in front of the television with the iron and singe the material when it got tense. She would rather have given the man a bill for the blouses right now. But rather than ironing, in this half hour by the Schlachtensee she had composed a letter to the man in Altena in her mind:

> My dear, when I gaze through other people's windows, when I copy the guests at other people's tables, turn away to carefully examine my own rough edges, when spiders dangle in front of my nose, scurry up invisible threads and eat small beetles, then and always I would like to be with you. With you, where everything is in soft focus. Your F.

She had piled up hundreds of such letters in her head. She didn't send any of them. Her yearning struck her as too delicate to be posted.

The man that the woman was meeting liked quoting lines.

He had studied in Oxford and was a good swimmer. The woman knew that. That's how she had first met him. He was wearing swimming goggles. His eyes were hidden. That had appealed to her. With 'You gave birth to me' the swimmer was citing a lyric by a shaven-headed female singer, where she talked about her baby. He wanted to use the text to explain to the woman how essential giving and taking were, and that taking was inherent in giving. In the moment of birth, woman gives something and simultaneously something is taken away from her, he said. The woman hated sentences with 'woman' in them. She had heard that the singer had lost custody of her child. The swimmer gratefully accepted the contribution. He was now lecturing her about the Anglo-Saxon legal system. The woman and the swimmer walked along the shore of the Schlachtensee. Suddenly the woman felt a familiar twinge in her hips. She had a stitch, but she wasn't out of breath. She knew what the stitch meant. She was getting bored. She put a hand to her waist. The twinge got worse. The swimmer didn't notice any of this. He was making an effort to ensure there were no silences in the conversation. The skin under his right eyebrow tensed. He could feel that his nervous tick would set in any second, an involuntary twitch underneath the eyelid. He spoke to keep it at bay. At the same time the woman's boredom was growing. She wasn't listening anymore, but she also couldn't think of anything of interest to relate either. She tried to suppress her boredom. She knew that this feeling was more dangerous than lust. She knew, too, that lust often arises out of boredom. She was glad that there was no roof arching over her. At least that way she would preserve decency. At a fork in the path where the water shimmered through the low hanging branches of the trees, the woman slipped her arm through the man's. The swimmer thought about it for fifty metres. Then he stood still and pulled the woman to him. The woman lifted her head. The twinge in her hips had grown stronger.

Today I kissed another man, the woman wrote to the man that evening. She didn't know how he would take it. She thought for a long time, and then continued:

He tasted of sour apples.

In answer: no, nothing should go on for ever. Nothing at all.

We can say much. Does that make it better? Here! Fall into my arms, give me the snakes and the dogs in your stomach, I shall coil them into chains, and I shall sing of thee and me, of us, to whom nothing is too ridiculous. Not revolutions, not prayer books, underpants with no elastic and cowardly viruses. That's fun. Fun is something that tingles in your fingertips when you dip your fingernails in it. It's a green liquid with bubbles.

The woman was exhausted after writing that. She had the feeling it hadn't come from her. She put the sheet of paper in her teaching folder and carried it around with her for a week. Then she chucked it away. She took it back out of the wastepaper bin. She sent the letter to the man, along with a train ticket. But the man let her wait. His mother was ill. The woman didn't think that was a good excuse. She had already forgotten the man at the Schlachtensee.

The man's mother was in a church-run hospital. But the man didn't see any nuns. He had the woman's letter in his pocket. He had already read it three times. He read it once more in the toilet. He liked the letter, it seemed so full of life. He decided to go to the woman the following weekend. The scene in the café the previous month struck him as unreal now. What was real was the promise in the letter, what he read between the lines. He saw it before him, the happiness yet to come, and he waved the letter in excitement, because otherwise he would have had to cheer. He only read what he wanted to read. He thought the other man that the woman mentioned was a joke. He went back to his mother's bedside.

She said she couldn't sleep in the hospital, there were noises all night long, the patients groaning, the night nurse with her boyfriend. After three days you start to see your own fingers as webbed, the hallucinations came from sleep deprivation. The man didn't tell his mother that he hadn't slept properly for ten years. He felt a slight draught in the nape of his neck and closed the window. While he yanked the lever he saw a prostitute on the other side of the street. It was raining. She was wearing platform boots, tight jeans and a lycra corset that sucked in her waist. Her hair looked like a long black carpet. When he drove off he took the girl with him. In the car park of a furniture shop she bent over him. When he put his hands in her hair she pushed him away.

At home he unpacked his luggage for the first time in weeks. The flat smelled funny. He flung the windows open, and noticed that they had grey streaks. He was too lazy to clean them. He collected the tortoise from the neighbour who had been looking after it and promised the student dinner. He would make spaghetti vongole, that would be quick. He wondered where he could buy the shellfish. As he came out of the student's flat into the hallway carrying the tortoise in his hand he saw the woman standing outside his door. She had jumped on a train. They looked at each other, the man with the reptile in his hand, the woman with a tired travelling face. But they didn't search the other's gaze, questions were superfluous. In the reflection of their desires they transformed themselves into the creatures in their letters, full of promises, riddles and secrets. They were their own angels. The woman said, 'I love you'. The man said, 'Me too'. Two days later they knew more.

ALSO AVAILABLE FROM COMMA...

The Silence Room

SEAN O'BRIEN

ISBN: 978 1905583171
RRP: £7.95

'Sean O'Brien does for libraries what Ursula Andress did for bikinis. Read and rejoice!' - Val McDermid

Chain-smoking alcoholics, warring academics, gothic stalkers and aspiring writers are just some of the visitors that browse the mysterious library at the heart of Sean O'Brien's fiction debut. Idlers and idolisers alike can be referenced, in body or in text, among the crepuscular alcoves and dim staircases of this seemingly unassuming building. The secret to a family curse, a dog-eared first edition of Stevens' Harmonium, the gruesome fate of a feminist literary theorist - all are available to simply take down from the shelf, as are the catalogue of genres and subject areas that O'Brien himself effortlessly deploys: from gothic horror to English pastoral, Critical Theory to Cold War noir.

'Sean O'Brien, like Graham Greene, creates his own instantly recognisable fictional landscape, where crime, mystery and disillusion lurk by the waters of the Tyne or Humber. His stories glint with black comedy and touches of the macabre and surreal. In O'Brien country you may hear the hoot of a train pulling out of the city, but you'll never be on it, because your place is here in the kingdom of backstreet pubs, tired, desirable girls and drowned men. Nothing is ever as it seems: it is much more frightening than that... First-class stories from one of our finest writers.' - Helen Dunmore

Under the Dam
and other stories

DAVID CONSTANTINE

ISBN: 0954828011
RRP: £7.95

'Flawless and unsettling'
Boyd Tonkin, Books of the Year, *The Independent*

'I started reading these stories quietly, and then became obsessed, read them all fast, and started re-reading them again and again. They are gripping tales, but what is startling is the quality of the writing. Every sentence is both unpredictable and exactly what it should be. Reading them is a series of short shocks of (agreeably envious) pleasure.'
- A S Byatt, Book of the Week, *The Guardian*

'A superb collection'- *The Independent*

'This is a haunting collection filled with delicate clarity. Constantine has a sure grasp of the fear and fragility within his characters.'
- A L Kennedy